For Jersey

Also by Scott Taylor

Chasing Your Tail (Silver Bow)

Screwed

by

Scott Taylor

720 Sixth Street, Box # 5
New Westminster, BC
CANADA V3L 3C5

Title: Screwed
Author: Scott Taylor
Cover Art: "Inner Sanctum Playground"
           painting by Candice James
Layout and Editing: Candice James
ISBN 9781774033210 (Print)
ISBN 9781774033227 (Ebook)
© 2024 Silver Bow Publishing

Library and Archives Canada Cataloguing in Publication

Title: Screwed / by Scott Taylor.
Names: Taylor, Scott (Author of Chasing your tail), author.
Identifiers: Canadiana (print) 20240462645 | Canadiana (ebook) 20240462718 | ISBN 9781774033234
   (softcover) | ISBN 9781774033241 (Kindle)
Subjects: LCGFT: Novels. | LCGFT: Humorous fiction.
Classification: LCC PS3620.A946 S37 2024 | DDC 813/.6—dc23

Screwed

The alarm went off, and he shot upright in bed.

"Shiiiiiiiiiiiiiitttttttttttttttt!" he screamed.

The thing kept going. All he had within reach was a balled-up sock, which he flung at the dresser. Nothing changed.

He got up and got dressed, went into the kitchen and made some breakfast. Cheerios and coffee. He had to find a job today, there was no choice. They were going to throw him out if he didn't.

Ralph finished eating and left the apartment. He got in the car and headed down the street towards the temp agency. It had been weeks, they had to have something for him by now.

The temp agency said that nothing was available. The bar down the street from the apartment building wasn't open yet. The place was called Willy's and was a total dive. Larry and Frank were both still at work, there was nothing to do. He drove around town aimlessly for awhile, just playing in traffic.

Around six, Larry came by and they went over to Willy's to get a drink. The girl next to him at the bar gave Ralph a sour look as he sat down next to her and ordered a beer. Ralph made a bad first impression.

And a second. And a third. He had gotten everything all wrong. He frowned when he was supposed to be smiling, and talked when he should shut up.

"Where's Frank?" he asked Larry, sipping his beer.

"Had to work overtime," Larry said. Frank worked stocking shelves at the supermarket, and Larry was a pizza delivery boy.

"We gotta get together this weekend, I have a new song I want to try out," Ralph said.

"Yeah ok, cool."

They had chugged the first round, and Henry the bartender came down to ask if they wanted another. The answer was yes, as always. Henry was an older fella, he was a nice guy.

They drank a few more beers and then they went home. The next day was Saturday, and Ralph was looking forward to band practice. The three of them had been in a band together for years, going all the way back to high school. Ralph played guitar and sang, Frank played bass and Larry was on the drums. None of them were any good, but they didn't know it yet.

The next morning, there was a squeal of tires and a muffled bump as Larry showed up at the apartment with Frank. A minute later there was a knock on the door and Ralph let them in.

"Did you hit the pole again?" Ralph asked Larry.

"Nah," Larry said.

Ralph looked at Frank. "He did, right?" Frank shook his head yes. Frank never spoke, he was a mute.

"Seriously, why can't you just drive the car?" Ralph asked, shaking his head. Larry was the worst driver in the world - every trip he made ended in near-disaster or worse. Frank didn't have a car, he rode a bike.

"Okay, so I got this new song. I came up with it in the shower the other day. It's really cool, you're gonna love it," Ralph said, sitting down on the ratty couch.

"Let's hear it," Larry said, sitting down across from him in the armchair.

Ralph walked them through the new song, showing them the beat and the chord changes. As usual, it was a simple thing with only about three chords total. Band practice was usually held there at Ralph's apartment. They couldn't make a lot of noise since the neighbors complained, so they had to just play unplugged and with no drums. They used to practice in Frank's mother's garage, but Ralph and Larry had pissed her off last time and they weren't allowed over there anymore.

"Okay, so where are we going to actually play this?" Larry asked pointedly.

Ralph glared at him. "I told you, I'm fucking working on it," he said, storming into the kitchen to get a beer. Larry gave him a skeptical grimace. Frank said nothing, as usual.

"I think I got us an audition with the guy at the place over on Melville," Ralph said as he came back in. He meant the bar near the center of town that had live music. "He said we could go down there next week and try out for him."

"I don't know what the point is, we never practice," Larry said. He went into the kitchen to get two more beers, one for him and one for Frank. Ralph never got them any, either because he was too oblivious or because he was an asshole. Probably both.

"I told you, I got something lined up. A guy I know said he can hook us up with a place out past the train tracks. It's in some old abandoned building or something. He said we could use it on the weekends."

Gina came over that night. Gina was Ralph's ex-girlfriend, and she was crazy. She was also as ugly as sin. She was rail thin with hair like straw and a tongue like sandpaper, like a small female scarecrow. Gina chain smoked, never ate, and drank all the time.

She walked into the apartment and sat down. "Get me a beer," she ordered, lighting up a cigarette. Upon being ignored, she went to the kitchen to get herself one.

"Where were you last night?" Ralph asked.

"At the Pinnacle, in the city," she said.

The Pinnacle was an upscale bar in Manhattan known for being a hangout for military guys. Gina worked as a secretary at an office nearby, but she was on a mission to become a full-time military wife. She desperately wanted to have kids but couldn't find anyone to have them with.

"With those same nitwit friends of yours?"

"They're not nitwits, you asshole."

"I mean, does this ever work? Do any of you ever pick someone up?" he asked, reclining on the couch with a smart-ass grin.

Gina didn't respon, just continued sucking on her cigarette nervously. Gina was neurotic as all hell - everything freaked her out. She was insecure and irritable.

"Why do you even want to be a military wife?" he asked her.

"I dunno, to travel around, see the world."

"They don't all travel, you know. You could get stuck in some bumblefuck place in Oklahoma for four years or something."

"Shut the hell up, what do you know about it."

Gina argued with everything Ralph said - it was the reason why they broke up. She had no interest in him anymore but for some reason she still wouldn't leave him alone. They had dated for about three months a while back, and everything about the situation had driven him nuts. She had a crazy dog that was always attacking him. It barked all the time, never shut up, and wouldn't listen to a thing he said.

"Sit the fuck down!" he would shout at it. It just kept barking.

He would sit in her living room with a beer, and from the kitchen she'd say 'This is the way it's going to be, when we're married...'

as if it was some euphoric, utopian thing already. He wasn't sure if that was the way he wanted it to be. Things went south quickly and he called it off. Gina got drunk all the time and would call him up and leave nasty messages on the answering machine.

***

"I know you're in there, bastard. Pick up the phone and talk to me..." she would seethe, her teeth grinding audibly. He could almost smell the alcohol through the machine.

Gina stayed for an hour, filled the room up with smoke, got bored and went home. Ralph was sure she only came over to torment him, because she knew how much it bothered him.

The next morning, he got in the car and went back over to the temp agency. Still nothing. Ralph had originally worked in IT, but the last job hadn't gone so well. He didn't have any references and it was fucking everything up. He went home again.

It was Friday night and they were going into Manhattan to go bar hopping. They lived in Caldwell, a town in Jersey about ten miles or so from the city. It was close to Route 80 and a bunch of other highways, but Ralph's car was an old beat-up tank and he didn't have any faith in its ability to get them there and back again. And he didn't trust Larry to drive anywhere, so they always took the train.

They got off in Penn Station and made a beeline for their favorite place, a run-down dive bar in Midtown called Roscoes. Larry tripped on the doorsill as they entered, almost going sprawling all over the place.

"How ya doin' Andy," Ralph said as they sat down, trying to ignore the klutz. Andy went to get the beers.

"That didn't take too long, to get in," Larry observed as the beer arrived. He took the mug and immediately spilled beer all down the front of his shirt as he went to drink it.

Ralph was getting irritable already. It tended to happen whenever Larry spoke, or did anything at all for that matter.

"Seriously, you need to start watching what you're doing. I don't know how you make it through the day," Ralph said sipping his beer.

"Whaddya want from me, shit happens," Larry said.

The song on the jukebox changed, it was now some country song.

"What's with the country?" Ralph yelled over at Andy.

"I didn't put it in," Andy said, rubbing a glass with a dishrag. "Bunch of morons came in before and loaded the thing up."

"Your Dad likes country, doesn't he?" Larry asked.

"Yeah, I grew up with it. I hate that shit," Ralph said.

"Nah, some of the old stuff's not bad."

They drank and looked around the place. There were a couple of derelicts at the other end of the bar, and a few patches of yuppies in the back.

"I'm thinking about driving a school bus," Ralph said.

"What?"

"A school bus, you know, for a job."

"What the hell you want to do that for?"

"For money, dipshit. The temp agency doesn't have anything anymore. It's easy work - and besides, I know a guy says he can get me in."

"That IT shit is a lot easier, I don't know why you don't go back to that again. At least it's in an office."

"I told you about that already."

"What?"

"I said 'I told you', my references are all screwed up. Because of all the assholes over there."

The real reason was that he had sat on his ass all day long doing nothing, but this never came to light in his discussions about it with people.

Ralph looked over Larry's shoulder, just to make sure Frank was still there. He was.

"Man it's dead in here," Ralph said glumly.

Larry was looking across the room, distracted. He turned back around. "What?"

"*DEAF* THING!!!" Ralph screamed. His whole face immediately went beet red. "I swear to God, if you say 'What' one more fuckin' time, I'm gonna throw this beer at you." He bent forward to look at Frank. "You can hear what I'm saying, right?" Frank nodded his head yes.

"Oh shut the fuck up," Larry said. "You need Prozac or something. Settle down, have a drink." He waved at the bartender. "Three shots of Jack, Andy."

Ralph's friend made the call and within days he'd gotten the job driving the school bus. Every day for a week, he took the kids back and forth in the big yellow thing. They were twelve and thirteen for the most part and thoroughly obnoxious. They all yelled and screamed the entire time, squawking like birds and generally causing trouble wherever possible. Traffic was horrible, people drove like idiots and it took him forever to get anywhere. Ralph gritted his teeth and made it through to the weekend.

By Monday of the second week, he'd had enough. The insolent little fucker sitting in the seat right behind him would not shut up, no matter how many times Ralph told him to quit. He was practically screaming right in his ear the whole way and it was driving him insane. Ralph turned around in his seat at the stop sign to face the kid.

"Listen to me - I'm going to wring your neck," he told him.

The kid laughed. "You're not gonna do anything, you jerkoff," he said. Ralph made to grab for the kid's shirt when he heard a voice from outside the bus. It was the crossing guard, who was standing on the sidewalk looking in through the window.

"Hey, you can't talk to the kids like that," she protested in a shrill, singsong voice.

Ralph took one look at her and knew his goose was cooked. He got the call after he got home from work that day - he was fired.

"How the hell do you get fired after only one week," Larry laughed into the phone when Ralph told him.

"Try driving that fucking bus and get back to me," Ralph countered furiously and hung up.

In the morning, he called his mother. It was something he tried to do every so often, even though it rarely (if ever) yielded positive results. His mother was a highly strung woman with a penchant for hysterical screeching, while his father was part of the furniture. He rarely spoke and when he did, it was usually just to say 'Listen to your mother...' His parents lived in the area but Ralph almost never saw them.

"Well look who it is..." his mother said sarcastically. "Did you call your sister?"

"No Ma, I didn't get to it yet," Ralph said, closing his eyes and bracing himself for the ordeal.

"I thought I told you to call her! Why didn't you do it?"

"I know, I'll call her today."

"Did you get a job yet? You know you need to get a job."

"Yeah, I had one, but I lost it again."

"YOU *HAD* ONE? WHAT DO YOU MEAN, YOU HAD ONE? WHAT HAPPENED??"

She'd started already. Ralph was hungover and couldn't take it, he hung up the phone before his head could explode.

Larry and Frank came by after dinner.

"I got us the practice space," Ralph told them as they sat around the kitchen table. "It's in that abandoned building I was telling you about, the one out past the train tracks. We should go over there on Sunday and check it out."

"What I'm more interested in is how you managed to lose that new job of yours so fast. How'd that happen? Huh? Huh?" Larry said. He was reaching across and poking Ralph in the arm repeatedly as he said it, trying to piss him off. And it was working.

As often happened, Ralph started picturing things taking place in his head. He imagined himself suddenly reaching out to grab Larry's wrist and pinning it to the table with one hand, and then bringing a huge mallet around in a wide swooping arc to smash it with the other. Instead, he just grabbed ahold of Larry's incoming finger and twisted. Larry howled. There was a short pause, as Frank looked on impassively.

"No seriously, what happened with the job?" Larry asked, resuming the conversation.

"The kids were fucking around, they made too much noise," Ralph said, swigging his beer. "Screw it, I'll get another one."

On Saturday Ralph went into the city to see his bookie. He went in once or twice a month to bet on the baseball games, despite the fact that he never won a bet. He'd been betting for years and it just never happened. It was almost spooky how bad his luck was.

They met in a bar in Midtown, the usual spot. The bookie sat across the table from him with a vague look of trepidation.

"Look Ralph, I know this is none of my business, but... I don't know what the point is. I mean you never win, I mean ever."

"Just give me ten on the White Sox, and five on the Mets," Ralph said wearily.

On Sunday he met with the band to practice. It was in an old brick building in a shitty area on the outskirts of town, flanked by a factory on one side and a disused parking lot on the other. It was a dilapidated mess. The windows were broken and there were just a few bare bulbs hanging down.

"This place is a disaster," Larry said, looking around as he carried the bass drum in.

"Nah, it's not that bad. We needed a place to play and this is all there was," Ralph said.

"And it's hot as shit in here," Larry continued.

"Shut up," Ralph said.

Once they'd moved all the equipment in and set everything up, Ralph counted off and they launched right into the new song. The amps growled, Larry thumped along on the drums. He was always behind the beat or ahead of it or looking for it, anywhere but directly on top of it. It was like he was trying to avoid it. Frank wasn't much better. He had no natural ear for music and they had to show him the right notes to play, and even when they did he managed to miss them more often than he found them. Halfway through the song, Ralph stopped and waved them off, already frustrated. He walked over to the drum kit.

"Nice and easy on the beat, man. It doesn't have to be so fast, just a nice groove," he said.

"Groove my ass," Larry laughed, "You don't even know how to play the thing yourself."

"Look, I'm gonna shove that drum stick up your ass." He went to grab it, but Larry was too fast and pulled it away.

"You're so full of shit. It's always us, we're always the ones screwing up right? The fact is, you can't play guitar yourself. And while we're at it, you can't sing either. That's the fuckin' problem."

Ralph stormed out of the room and slammed the door. Practice was going about as well as it usually did.

The temp agency called on Monday, they had a job for him. It was a catering gig, helping to set stuff up at rich kids' birthday parties. He did it for a few days and it made him sick. All day long, carrying aluminum trays full of pasta and meatballs and laying out the Styrofoam plates and plastic utensils while the mothers preened and the brats carried on.

"What's with the jobs with kids," Larry asked later on in the apartment. "Whadd're you, strange?"

"I didn't ask for this one," Ralph growled. "But you know what, I'd rather work with kids anyway. It's better than the fucking adults, I can't handle them anymore."

"You can't handle kids either," Larry said. "I've seen you with them."

"Oh, shit... I almost forgot," Ralph said, brightening up. "We got that audition at the place over on Melville. The guy called me yesterday, we have to go down there and play for them on Wednesday afternoon."

"What the hell are we gonna play?" Larry asked. "We don't know anything."

"Yes we do. We can do the blues stuff."

Larry couldn't remember ever having done any of the 'blues stuff' properly in practice either, but he didn't feel like having an argument.

On Wednesday they drove over. It was a rinky-dink little hole-in-the-wall place that didn't even have a stage. They carted their stuff in and set up in the corner by the big plate glass window in front. The old man looked hard of hearing - in fact, he looked like he might fall over at any moment. They ran through a couple of quick blues numbers, practically bludgeoning them to death but making it through to the end without anything dreadful happening. The kid working the kitchen came out during the second song to sneer at them from the back.

When they finished up, the old man just stood there staring at them. Ralph was about to ask him what he thought, when suddenly he came to life and rasped "Yeah yeah, we'll call you." Then he turned around and tottered into the back room. They packed the car up and went home.

Over at Willy's that night, they sat around discussing it.

"I thought it went okay," Ralph said, sipping at his beer.

"It went terrible," Larry said. "We suck. 'We'll call you' means only one thing."

"Shut the fuck up," Ralph said, waving his hand dismissively. "We just need a break. We have to find the right audience."

"The School for the Deaf is over in Clifton. Maybe we should try there," Larry said. He turned around. "What about you Frank, what did you think?"

Frank shrugged his shoulders. Apparently he didn't have an opinion.

***

It was the height of summer. The weather was hot, the days were long and they started looking around for something to do. Larry suggested that they take a fishing trip. Ralph had no idea why anyone would want to do such a thing. To Ralph, fishing was just the same as drinking beer except you had to hold a pole in one hand while you did it, it made no sense. But Larry was insistent that they would have a grand old time. They jumped in the car one morning, grabbed ahold of Frank and drove over to the lake. The parking lot was all gravel and Ralph was worried he'd pop a tire.

"Why can't they pave this shit," he groused as the stones growled beneath the wheels.

Ralph and Frank didn't even own fishing poles and so Larry had had to bring along a couple of extras for them. He took the poles out of the trunk, thrust them into their reluctant hands and turned around to blaze a trail forward. The mosquitos were out in force and Ralph was already slapping at his neck.

"What the hell are we doing here," he grumbled to himself.

They found a suitable spot along the shoreline and parked themselves in the grass. The folding chairs were aligned in a neat little row, worms were produced and lures cast into the water. Larry leaned back in his chair and sighed.

"Ahhh, the great outdoors. Look at that nice lake, all that open space," he said.

"Yeah, right," Ralph said.

He went right for the cooler and pulled out the first beer. If nothing else, he was going to get shitfaced.

An hour later, no one had caught anything. It was hotter than hell and the sun was beating down on them. Ralph was getting antsy, but trying hard to keep his mouth shut for once. If this was Larry's thing, then so be it. Finally he couldn't stand it anymore.

"Look, I'm tired of this. Who the fuck goes fishing anyway?"

"What's that supposed to mean," asked Larry, fixing him with a bellicose stare.

"Just what I said. If we want fish, we can get them at the supermarket. Why do we have to sit here getting eaten alive trying to pull them out of the fuckin' lake."

"Because it's relaxing," Larry countered.

"It's not relaxing, it's about to drive me over the edge."

"Real men fish. This is what guys do. What the fuck is wrong with you."

"People who lack imagination fish. Vegetables and subnormals fish. It's an activity for mental patients. Frank, are you enjoying this?" Ralph asked. Frank was asleep. Ralph got up to take a piss behind a tree.

Another half-hour and Larry felt a nibble on the line. He reeled it in and it was a tiny little sunfish. Ralph glared at it grimly.

"*That's* what we've been waiting for? What are you going to do with that, feed it to the cat?"

"Seriously, you bitch like an old woman," Larry said. "Go get your fish at the supermarket and shut the fuck up."

"I'll tell you what I'm gonna to do - I'm gonna put this pole back in the trunk and go get a quarter-pounder from McDonalds, that's what I'm gonna do," Ralph jibed.

"Good for you, you do that," Larry said. "You know what I'm gonna do? I'm gonna take this pole and shove it up your ass, how bout that."

"Go ahead and try it."

"I'm gonna do it."

"Go ahead."

They sat there staring at each other for awhile. Then Ralph looked over at Frank, who was now slumped in his chair and beginning to snore.

"How can he sleep through all that?" he asked.

"Kid has a clean conscience," Larry said. "He can sleep through anything."

"Come on, seriously, I'm gonna die from boredom. Let's get the hell out of here, let's go to Willy's."

The next weekend they decided to go down to Great Adventure to ride some roller coasters. Down the Parkway they went on a Saturday morning in Ralph's piece of shit Oldsmobile, praying that it would survive the trip. They parked the car, headed through the gate and went to find some beers to drink beforehand. The last part was Larry's idea.

"What the fuck are we doing going to Great Adventure?" Larry said, shaking his head as they walked through the crowd.

"This is payback for the fishing, isn't it. Whadd're you talking about, you don't like roller coasters?" Ralph asked.

"No," Larry replied.

"Why not?"

"They're boring."

"And *fishing* isn't? Bullshit, you're scared."

"My ass."

But the beer went down Larry's throat awfully fast that morning, as they sat there in the cafeteria surrounded by parents with their heavy cameras dangling and little kids eating their ice cream.

The sun was hot and the lines were long. Finally they got to the front of one of them. It was a big tall bastard that went up a steep incline before dropping off into a canyon of crazy twists and turns. They climbed in three across, with Frank in the middle seat. The ride rumbled to life, the cars began to climb up the slope and Larry didn't look at all well. When they reached the top, the lead car hung in midair for just a short second before plummeting clear off the face of the earth. Larry started to shriek like a little baby. He hadn't had enough beer.

"Holy crap, my ears," Ralph said, listening to Larry's cries of death as the coaster careened toward the bottom of the first valley. He looked over at Frank to see how he was making out. Frank's eyes were closed and there was a blissful smile on his face; he was as free as a bird as the sun shone down and the wind went whipping through his hair. Sometimes Ralph wondered if Frank had been a Buddhist monk in a past life.

A few more beers and they were able to coax Larry onto another couple of rides, albeit far less stressful ones. Then when they'd had enough, they headed back in the evening.

The new job lasted two weeks this time. In the beginning it was okay and Ralph just went in and did his time. One morning however, he went in hungover as hell and things started to slip. The mothers were being particularly demanding and the brats all had loud mouths. His normally limited patience was nonexistent that day. One of the kids was running behind him as he carried out a heavily laden tray, nipping at his heels and making a nuisance of himself. Ralph looked around to see if any adults were within earshot.

"It's a good thing your mother isn't here right now..." he whispered at the kid, shooting him a look. The kid laughed and kept right on doing what he was doing.

Ralph put the tray down and went to go back for another one. A little girl next to him screeched.

"Shut the fuck up," he said under his breath. This time, a mother heard it.

"Did you just tell my daughter to shut up?" she asked indignantly, putting her hands on her hips.

"No," Ralph lied.

"Yes you did, I heard you do it." She immediately sashayed off to find the appropriate authority figure to complain to.

So Ralph had been fired again. He came home, threw the keys on the table and went for a beer. Outside, his next-door neighbor slammed her car door.

"God damn bitch," he said.

Ralph decided to make another try for an IT job. He sent resumes around to a bunch of companies and sat around waiting. Every now and then, one of them responded and he would get an interview. The interviews went badly. The smug little bastards liked to talk down to him and insult him in a variety of underhanded ways. He sat there imagining how delicious it would be to suddenly just give the interviewer a huge middle finger, eyebrows arching as he stuck it way up in the air, and then wait to see what reaction it would produce. He wanted to take the finger and wave it in the guy's face, stick it up his nose, push him backwards off his little swivel chair and shove him clear out the window with it. But that would land us in jail, so we didn't do that. Ralph had always figured that someday he would wind up in jail - in fact, he was kind of surprised he hadn't made it there yet.

So he spun his wheels during the day, driving around town for no reason and wondering what to do with himself. His mother called one night and invited him over for dinner. He went.

"So, where have you been??" his mother demanded as he sat down on the couch across from his father.

"Same place I'm always at," Ralph said.

"You never call, you never come over - what are you, too good for us?" she said.

"No Ma, I'm just busy."

"Still hanging out with those crazy friends of yours I'll bet. You know that I think your friend Frank is a little off."

"Nah, he just doesn't like to talk."

"He doesn't make a sound," his father interjected. "He's retarded."

"Have you called your sister yet?" his mother asked.

"No Ma, I haven't called her yet."

"Why not? I thought I told you to call! She's having a hard time right now, she's your sister and she could use a little support!"

"Okay, fine," Ralph said, trying to breathe slowly.

"Listen to your mother," his father said, not looking up from his paper.

"You know we got in a fight again the other night. There's just no talking to her, she's always yelling and screaming. I can't get a word in edgewise when she's in one of her little moods."

His mother went on for fifteen minutes about it. She was constantly fighting with everyone, but somehow nothing was ever her fault. She loved to argue as long as she was winning. As soon as she started to lose however, she would immediately announce 'I have a headache!' and no one was allowed to talk anymore.

"Have you gone to the doctor yet?" his mother asked, once she'd finished her first harangue.

"No Ma, it's not bothering me as much anymore," Ralph replied.

"Well you still should go, you never know until you get it tested. And you need a new doctor, you were saying that you didn't trust him and you need a good doctor, nothing is more important. I don't know why you don't listen to me. No one ever listens to me."

"Okay, that's enough. Seriously, and you wonder why I never come over here."

"What's the matter? I didn't do anything. What's the problem, what did I say?" she whined. She turned to his father. "George, say something. What did I say, did I say anything? It doesn't call for that kind of attitude. All I did was ask him about the doctor and he got like he always does, it's the same exact thing you do..."

"Oh boy," his father moaned in a tired voice, trying to disappear into the chair. It was his other favorite line. Ralph got up to go to the bathroom, just to escape.

They ate dinner, his mother nagged him for another hour and then he went home. There was a message from Gina waiting on the machine. He deleted it without listening to it and went to bed.

On Saturday night they were going over to Willy's. Gina called again.

"I want to go with you guys, come on!"

"No Gina, you can't come."

"Why not?"

"Because you're a pain in the ass."

He hung up the phone to the sound of squealing tires outside, followed by a thump. Larry had arrived.

They drove over in Ralph's car, parked in front of the bar and went in. Over the entrance, the sign was starting to come loose from its moorings and looked about ready to fall off the wall.

They sat down in the usual spot. The place was pretty packed, a lot more people in there than usual.

"Henry, the sign's coming down out front," Larry yelled down the bar.

"No shit sherlock," Henry yelled back.

They drank a few beers and shots and looked around the place. The music was blasting on the jukebox and there was a long wait list for the pool table. A young pretty girl was sitting to Ralph's right. She glanced over at him for a second.

"How ya doin'," he said.

"Not too bad," she replied.

"You guys come here often?" he asked with a smile.

"You serious?" she said. She turned back around to talk to her friends, giving him the cold shoulder of death. Ralph went back to his beer.

"Nice job there, Romeo," Larry said in his ear.

"Shut the fuck up," Ralph said.

The weeks went by and summer dragged along. Frank started working a lot of overtime so the Three Amigos weren't together as often as usual. It was hot as hell outside so Ralph spent most of the time inside, hiding in the air conditioning.   He watched a lot of porn and jerked off to pass the time, sometimes as often as three times a day. It wasn't a habit he was terribly proud of, but what the hell, he was only human.

Gina came over on a weeknight, drunk at 9 pm and pounding on the door like the police. Ralph let her in.

"What the hell," he said.

Gina didn't bother asking for a beer, she just went in and got herself one.

"I had a date on Friday night," she said, coming in and sitting down next to him as she lit up a cigarette.

"Oh yeah, how did that go."

"Horrible. What a loser, you should have seen him. Skinny little fucker, still lived at home with his mom. Couldn't even look me in the eye."

"What happened to the pilots, can't find any?"

"Dunno, I haven't seen them around lately. Who cares, they always go running off with the fucking blondes anyway. With their goddamn short skirts." Gina took a long swig of her beer. "Why do you buy this light shit, it's disgusting."

"Keeps the stomach down," Ralph replied, taking his own slug.

Gina leaned back into the cushions and gave him what she thought was a seductive look. "What about us, you think we should give it another try?" She smiled, watching him through half-closed, beer-goggling eyes.

"Oh, Gina," Ralph muttered. "You know the way it goes." He looked at her in all sincerity for once, thought about saying more and pulled up short.

"Wonder what's on TV," he said, grabbing the clicker.

***

Larry was over the next day, lying on the couch watching TV.

"I have to go to the supermarket to get some food," Ralph said, grabbing his keys and heading for the door.

"I'll come with you," Larry said.

They walked into the store and Ralph headed for the frozen food aisle, with Larry leaning into him yapping in his ear the whole time. Larry was obsessed with some girl at work and he would not stop talking about it.

He went on and on, about how hot this chick was, how much he wanted to bang her yadda yadda yadda while Ralph put cans of soup and boxes of pasta into the little basket.

He got everything he needed and headed for the front. Larry was like a riveting gun, there was just no turning him off. Ralph started to get rattled. He felt his nerves fraying and his hands beginning to shake.

"Larry, you've gotta stop talking," he said under his breath as they approached the checkout counter. The little girl was standing there with a fake smile on her face. Ralph reached into the basket just as Larry leaned into him for about the tenth time, making him drop the frozen dinner box on the conveyor belt.

"Dude, stop," Ralph urged. The girl kept smiling. Ralph glared at her. He went into the basket again and this time he dropped a can of soup right on his foot.

A few cans later, Larry was still talking and Ralph was about to lose it. His head felt hot and there was a buzzing in his ears. The girl was now watching them with poorly concealed distaste. Ralph went for the last can in the basket, and once again it slipped out of his fingers and went rolling on the floor. He and Larry reached to grab it at the same time and butted heads, going down in a heap together. Ralph tried to get up, but there was a wet patch on the floor and as he slipped on it he grabbed for the counter, snagging the edge of the frozen box of food and bringing it down on top of him. Ralph climbed to his feet. The stars were bursting in his head. He reared back and let it go.

"Fuckkkkkkkkkk!!" he screamed.

The entire store was now paying close attention. A security guard materialized and walked up to them.

"Is there a problem, sir?" he asked. They looked at each other for awhile. There most certainly was, but he wasn't sure if there was anything the guard could do about it.

Another week passed. There were no jobs, there was nothing to do. It was too hot to go outside and Larry was being a pain in the ass so he didn't even feel like going out to get a beer. He drank in the apartment instead, by himself, staring at the wall and counting the seconds. He watched the baseball games at night and tried to give a shit.

Finally, Ralph got a call - the impossible had happened, he'd gotten a job. It was with some behemoth corporation over in Parsippany, one of these master-of-the-universe places with a fancy corporate campus and security and the whole big production. He'd lied about the references, but apparently no one had bothered to check on them. In fact, about half the resume had been bullshit. But none of that mattered anymore: he was through the door, home free. He was to start first thing Monday morning.

He rose to the sound of the horrible alarm, got all dressed up in his best 'business casuals', got in the car and left. In order to get to work, it would be necessary to fight his way up Route 80. Route 80 was possibly the worst highway in the world. It was one long continuous stream of traffic stretching from New York all the way into Pennsylvania. It may have stretched clear to California for all he knew. It was a certified nightmare which struck fear in Ralph's heart every time he had to endure it.

The cars were a maddening ribbon of oozing traffic that morning, everyone snarled together and going nowhere. You could feel the frustration wafting from the cars all around. Ralph turned the radio up louder and waited. Route 80 gradually merged into Route 287, a whole lot more aggravation and then he'd made it to the exit. Ralph found the campus, buzzed in at the security gate and soon was standing before his new home away from home - his cubicle. It was a tiny little space, remarkably similar to all the others. A chair, a monitor, bright lights and little walls on all sides. Looked like fun.

Soon Ralph met his new boss, a man named Mr. Davis. Mr. Davis was tense. About as tense as you could be. He had a raging case of OCD and nothing was ever satisfactory.

'"NO!!! THAT'S WRONG!!!" he would scream every time Ralph went near the keyboard. Mr. Davis' face would turn crimson and he would start sweating profusely. The man was under some serious pressure. Ralph's imagination took ahold of him - to amuse himself, he pictured Mr. Davis shrieking like a tea kettle until he spontaneously combusted, exploding all over the office in a shower of organic material. Life was sure to be a hoot working under Mr. Davis.

Sitting next to Ralph was a slothful creature named Boris, who almost never moved. He was pudgy and dull-looking, with big jowls and strands of thinning hair. A huge plant sat next to him in the cube. Even if Boris was given work to do, he would just sit there in an almost catatonic state, refusing to budge. Ralph wondered if it was deliberate, or if the guy was simply incapable of motion. Every so often, he would watch him surreptitiously from over the top of the divider. Boris would take the stapler and move it around the desk, placing it in different positions, moving it this way and that, just so. It was about all they could get him to do, and yet they never fired him. Supposedly he'd been working there forever, too - maybe he had dirt on someone, who knew.

The chick on the other side gave Mr. Davis a run for his money in the tension department. Debbie was high strung and nervous, snapping at anyone who ventured within range. She looked constantly on the edge of a nervous breakdown, and Ralph wondered how many she'd had already. He was surrounded by mental cases. It was only a matter of time before he went postal and started offing them left and right.

The saving grace there at work was a guy by the name of Max. He was a young kid like Ralph, another smartass but one who was dry and deadpan. Max had gone to a good school and actually gotten a degree in computer science and the whole nine yards. He and Ralph had hit it off immediately and were soon joined at the hip. Ralph was relieved that there was at least one sane person to talk to in the entire place.

There was an Indian guy down the hall that they had frequent interactions with. Udarsh spoke with a fairly heavy accent, which for the life of him Ralph could not understand. Everyone else there seemed to have no trouble with it, but for Ralph it might as well have been Swahili.

Udarsh would go on at length about a particular topic, and then Ralph would be obliged to respond. There would be a long pause.

"...What?" Ralph would say, incredulously. Udarsh would stand there glaring at him.

"Look, everyone else here understands what I'm trying to say," he would say, his voice rising in indignation. "I don't know what your problem is."

Ralph would just stare back at him with barely concealed contempt, then look around as if to see if anyone else might have caught the latest broadcast.

Ralph dragged himself to Parsippany every day and tried not to get fired. So far, so good: despite the perpetual ravings of Mr. Davis and friction with the other assorted loonies, nothing dreadful had happened yet and he was managing to keep his head above water. He and Max went to lunch together every day in the cafeteria, huddled together to commiserate when they could and generally tried to ignore everyone and everything else as much as possible.

***

Meanwhile the band kept practicing. Ralph was trying to get something down on tape using an old recorder he'd found buried in the closet, so they'd have a demo of some kind to pass around to people. They were struggling painfully through Ralph's songs, seldom surviving to the end of one of them without the whole thing completely falling apart.

"Larry - what the hell are you doing? That's way too fuckin' slow," Ralph said, taking his guitar off and chucking it on a chair.

"It's not too fuckin' slow, you just can't play guitar. What are you, deaf? Can you not hear what I'm doing?" Frank sat down in the corner to wait it out, munching on a candy bar.

"Every time it's the same thing with you - I've showed you how to do it like ten fuckin' times already. Why can't you just play the thing the right way?"

"I AM playing it right, you moron, I just told you."

"My left dick. You've got shit for brains, that's the problem."

"Bullshit."

"Go shove it up your mother's ass!"

"Shove it up your OWN mother's ass!"

The two of them got creative when things became heated. There was some sort of sick poetry going on there. Ralph and Larry bickered for another hour and then they went home. No demos were recorded that day.

They went to play a second audition, which went even worse than the first one. The place was over in a bad part of town, going out toward Newark.

"How the hell did you find this place," Larry said from the back seat.

"Tony at the bar told me about it, the creepy guy. He said the owner was looking for people."

"And they know we're coming?"

"Yeah, I called them."

They pulled up. It was a roadhouse bar kind of joint, a spacious room with a wraparound bar and a dance floor and a big stage. The owner was a young guy with slicked back hair who wore sunglasses and looked like he was full of shit. They got up on the stage, plugged in and started fumbling through the set. They played even worse than usual, actually stopping in the middle of the second song because Ralph broke a string and went to pieces because of it. The owner stood there smirking, trying to decide if he even needed to suppress the laugh.

"I think we have to go back to the blues stuff, and only play that from now on," Ralph said in the car on the way back.

"Bullshit, that stuff sucks. Anyways we haven't even played it for like years," Larry said.

"Yeah, but at least we can play it. We're never gonna get anywhere if we can't even make it through the fuckin' song. Frank, what do you think?" Frank shrugged his shoulders, he was noncommittal.

"I need a beer," Ralph said.

"Yeah, let's go to Willy's."

It was Wednesday night, after work. His mother called again.

"I wish you hadn't run off like that the other night, there were other things I wanted to talk to you about," she said.

"I didn't run off, I just had to go," Ralph replied.

"Your father and I got in another fight again... He's always getting angry at me, I wish you'd say something to him about it." Ralph said nothing, using the expectant pause to drink his beer instead.

"Well, are you going to talk to him?" she demanded.

"Yeah Ma, I'll talk to him." He had no intention of doing any such thing, but it held back the dam for a while longer.

"I don't know why it's a problem, I just need you to say something to him, he's just impossible, he never speaks and when he does it's always just to argue with me..."

"I told you, I'll talk to him."

"Well is it a problem? Why are you getting an attitude?"

"I don't have an attitude Ma, what are you talking about."

"What, I'm not allowed to talk to you about this?"

Ralph's head was beginning to hurt. His forehead was warm and the little stars were starting to dance around in front of his eyes.

"What do you want me to say?"

"I just want you to talk to him! Tell him that you think he treats me unfairly. And tell him that your sister says the same thing." Ralph took another swig.

"Are you listening to me?"

"Yeah Ma, I'm listening."

"Well then why don't you say something?!"

"How many times do I have to say the same thing?"

"Well you're not answering me! I wish you'd just listen to me. I'm always saying the same thing, no one ever listens."

"I'm listening."

"He's been like this for years, and no one ever helps me with him. You've got to tell your father what I told you. I just can't get through to him. I try to talk to him and he just sits there and doesn't say anything, and then he gets mad at me and it's the same thing all over again."

"Okay, sounds good."

"Well what's with the attitude? Why do you always have to get like that? Do you agree with me?"

"Absolutely, Ma."

"Well then why won't you *help* me? If you agree with me then just say something to him!"

"You bet."

"When are you going to tell him?"

"The next time I talk to him."

"Why don't you talk to him now. I'll put him on the phone and you can tell him right now."

"No, I'd rather not."

"But why not? If you agree with me then why don't you just do it now?"

"No, I'll tell him next time."

"*See?* You never help me! Why don't you just *say something* to him?"

"I'm going to."

"I mean, is it a big deal? Like we never help you with anything? When I ask you for something it always has to be - "

It was all he could handle, he hung up the phone. Ralph wasn't sure if all women on Earth were shrews, but nine out of ten of the ones in his life were. Maybe it was just New Jersey. He doubted it though.

***

Another alarm went off. Time for work again. Ralph drank three cups of coffee and still couldn't wake up. He was half asleep as he drove through the crowded streets of Caldwell, making his way toward Route 80. A huge bus suddenly veered into his lane, swerving way over the line and just about sideswiping him. Ralph was too tired to care.

"Fuckin' bus..." he muttered, as an afterthought.

At the office, he was met with a pleasant surprise - Mr. Davis had been transferred to another department. His replacement, and Ralph's new boss, had called a meeting to make introductions. They all gathered around the big table in the conference room to wait for him. He walked in shortly after.

The new boss was extremely tall and gaunt. He had dark features, dark eyes, dark hair - the man was dark, he looked like gloom personified. When he spoke it was with a deep, raspy voice, like some corpse risen from the dead and trying to communicate with the living.

"Dude looks like the Grim Reaper," Max whispered behind his hand. Ralph immediately pictured him as a bony skeleton, wearing a long black robe and carrying a scythe.

"It's wonderful to meet all of you. I am extremely excited to accept this new challenge, and to have the opportunity to work with a whole new group of wonderful people," the boss wheezed, smiling as he stood stiffly in front of the group.

"At least he sounds like a nice guy," Ralph remarked.

Ralph went to lunch by himself that day, as Max had to run to the bank. At the elevator on the way back, a woman was coming out just as he was going in. She was dressed to kill, all dolled up in the usual corporate attire, with rings and necklaces and severe makeup and hair done just so. He stepped aside politely to let her pass. She glared at him with steely eyes as she went by, looking down her nose at him like he was the help or something. Ralph lost it. He gave her the finger behind her back as she strode off, shaking it violently at her. He gave her the finger so hard, the finger almost fell off. Ralph looked across the lobby - there was a janitor over by the wall, watching him with great curiosity as he danced around fuming with his finger stuck in the air. Ralph stopped what he was doing and got in the elevator.

In the afternoon, Udarsh came by to discuss the project they were working on. He was going on at length in the usual way. Ralph stared at him blankly, growing impatient.

"C'mon, what, what?" Ralph said cutting him off, almost gritting his teeth.

"What do you mean 'what', you stupid bastard, I know you know what I'm saying. Don't start with that shit," Udarsh shot back.

"No one understands a thing you're trying to say," Ralph said. Max stepped in to defuse the situation.

"Indeed I grasp your meaning perfectly, good sir. We shall set to work forthwith." Max liked to get high-falutin' sometimes. His family had money and he had graduated from some fancy school upstate. He read a lot and knew all sorts of crazy shit. Meanwhile, Ralph and Udarsh continued with their staring contest, glowering back and forth.

"Can we gather from the latest announcement that he has the specs ready?" Ralph asked Max.

"Yeah of course I have the specs ready motherfucker, you know that because you heard it just fine the first time," Udarsh spat, bouncing up and down with indignation.

Ralph looked at him for a while longer, letting the sounds float by. "Why do you even bother?" he asked, shaking his head.

Udarsh went to say something further, then turned and stormed off instead. The muffled sound of frustrated Indian drifted down the hall.

Ralph went home after work, took a beer out of the fridge and sat down on the couch. The clicker was next to him but he didn't feel like watching TV. He sat there, staring into space. Work sucked, and then you came home and were rewarded with nothing to do. Ralph began to daydream. He imagined what it would be like to just get up and walk out the door, drop everything and leave, get in the car and just go. Ralph didn't know where he'd go though. Maybe to California. Or Canada.

***

Larry called on Sunday, around lunchtime.

"I'm coming over," he said.

"Why?" Ralph said. There was a dial tone. Larry was on his way, there was no stopping it. Ralph puttered around in advance of the inevitable. He waited for the sound of fender slamming into pole, then got up to open the door.

"Goddamn traffic. I'm tellin' ya, it's getting worse," Larry said, heading for the fridge.

"Where's Frank?" Ralph asked.

"He's at church," Larry said from the kitchen.

"He goes to church?"

"Yeah he's religious, his mother drags him along. You didn't know he goes to church?"

"Dunno, maybe I did."

"You're oblivious to everything."

"Listen," Ralph said as Frank came back in, "we need to start practicing more, we have to take it more seriously. This once a week crap isn't going to cut it anymore."

"I got news for ya pal, we're not going anywhere no matter how much we practice. It's time you faced reality," Larry said, chugging half his beer in one gulp as he did so.

"The hell are you talking about?"

"We're not any good. And we never get any better. You have to call it like you see it."

"Bullshit."

"Nope, it's the truth."

They both sat there drinking their beer. Ralph steamed in silence for awhile.

"Well if you don't fucking like it, then you should just quit," Ralph suddenly blew up.

"Nah, it's way too much fun pissing you off," Larry replied. He went rummaging around for the remote. "The Mets game is on, isn't it?"

"Fuck the Mets and fuck you," Ralph said.

Larry left when the game was over. The Mets won 5-2. They'd drank about a half a case each. Ralph was pissed. What the hell did he mean, 'We're not any good'? Larry could speak for himself. One of these days, they were going to get their act together, Ralph could feel it in his bones. He spent the rest of the night pacing around the apartment, fuming impotently. The phone rang at ten. He answered it.

"What??" he growled.

"I'm coming over," Gina said. Jesus Christ, between her and Larry.

"No you're not," he fired back.

"Yes I am," she replied.

"Gina, if you come over here I'm leaving," Ralph told her.

"Where are you going?" she asked. He hung up.

＊＊＊

It was Monday morning. Ralph couldn't handle it, he called in sick. He thought about going into the city to see his bookie and place a few bets but he didn't have the energy to deal with the city. Instead he got in the car and drove around town. There was a new coffee place on the corner near the movie theater - he stopped in to get a coffee, just for something to do. The barista looked at him like he'd just passed gas. Everyone was always glaring at something. He took his coffee and went to the park with it. Old men sitting with their dogs, children feeding pigeons. The adults were all busy slaving away. There were never any signs of life during the day.

He sat on the bench to think things over. The band had to get its ass in gear, if it didn't his head was going to cave in. They'd been screwing up for long enough already - something had to change. They needed to practice more, that was all there was to it. If Larry didn't like it, he could go fuck himself. Ralph spent half the morning thinking about it, it was all he could think of.

He got up and walked around, going in big pointless circles around the park. Then he went to the drive-thru at McDonalds to get lunch and took it back home. Willy's was about to open, but he didn't feel like going. There was a place over in Hackensack he had gone a few times, a place called Lydia's that had really good-looking girls working there. He hadn't been there in a while and he needed a change of pace, so he went over.

Lydia's hadn't changed at all since last time. It was a long narrow joint, like a railroad car, with a bar that stretched almost the entire length. A bunch of day drinkers sat here and there, working at their beers and not saying too much. The bartenders were all still hot as hell. The owner knew his business, it was worth going in there just to watch them walk back and forth. They all wore skimpy little shorts and tight T-shirts with their tits popping out - it was almost like going to Hooters, better than Hooters in fact. When they came to ask if you wanted another round, there was only one answer possible. There was almost no way to tear yourself away from them. Ralph sat there all afternoon, eating pretzels and chugging beer and gawking at the girls as they strutted behind the bar. The sun went down and he kept going. A couple of young kids came in, whooping it up and settling in to shoot some pool, regulars by the sound of it. Ralph thought about putting some quarters down but he didn't feel like putting up with the hassle. He watched people come and go. When he was hungry, he ordered a hamburger and fries from the grill and wolfed it down. Hamburgers were all he'd eaten since he'd gotten out of bed that morning. It was one of those days.

He got back in the saddle and went to work the next morning. The week flowed by like mud, but eventually it ended. It was Friday night and they were going into the city. On the way out of the subway, Larry came up alongside Ralph to show him something.

"Look what I got," Larry said, almost giggling. He had a little baggie full of powder in his hand.

"What the hell is that? Where did you get it?" Ralph asked.

"It's speed," Larry said. "Got it off a guy at work."

They didn't usually do drugs - every once in a while when it was dangled under their noses, but it was pretty rare. They pushed their way through the door into Roscoes. The place was slammed, it was wall-to-wall people in there.

"Hey Frank, Larry got some speed. You want some?" Ralph said in Frank's ear, struggling to make himself heard above the noise as they sidled up to the bar. Frank nodded his head yes. He didn't need to think about it.

One at a time, they went into the bathroom to do some of the stuff. After about a half hour, it started to hit them. Suddenly Larry was babbling like a Thai hooker and twitching like a bird. There was a new girl working the bar that night, someone they hadn't seen before. Larry grabbed her by the arm as she went by.

"What's your name?" he asked feverishly, practically panting.

"Pauline," she said, frowning and pulling her arm away.

"'Pauline' - that's a great name!! That's the best name I've ever heard!!" The girl walked away in utter disgust. Larry wheeled around to face Ralph again.

"Pauline!" he shouted. Larry didn't handle his liquor too well, and apparently he handled his drugs even worse.

Soon they were all amped up. Ralph was now talking way too much himself and bothering everyone around him. Frank was so wired he looked ready to speak. He got up off the stool, walked across the room and started to dance with a couple of young chicks who were standing over by the jukebox. They smiled at him and threw their hands in the air, hooting and hollering. Frank danced around in little circles, that familiar blissful smile plastered all over his face.

Ralph tried to talk to the chick next to him and was roundly ignored. Suddenly Larry was in his face again.

"PAULINE!!!" Larry screamed.

"What the fuck," Ralph said, wiping the spray of beer off his face.

They stayed out all night long. When Roscoes closed, they ambled over to a late night bar that stayed open until four, then they headed for the cafeteria on Third Avenue to drink some coffee and try to straighten up. A bunch of homeless guys were laying about the place, wearing overcoats and snoring loudly. Ralph was still reeling from the shit they'd taken earlier and didn't feel at all right. His heart was pounding, his eyes were twitching and his head felt like it was on fire. He doubted he would sleep for days.

Larry was still going. "Pauline, Pauline, Pauline..." he was whispering to himself in a goofy little singsong voice.

"Dude, I'm gonna have to commit you," Ralph said. "Relax."

Frank had danced the night away with whoever let him, and was just now starting to come down. He sat slouched in the booth, sipping his coffee and looking out the plate glass window with a perplexed look on his face, as if trying to figure out what had just happened to him. The sun had come up, the city denizens were slowly emerging from their hiding places.

They sat there for an hour. "Shit, I'm hungry," Ralph said. "Let's go over to that diner a few blocks up."

"What's wrong with the food here?" Larry asked.

"Nah, I want an omelet. Come on."

They got out of there and went a few blocks up. The diner was just opening up, but it already had a few customers. It was a beat-up, seedy place with ripped red swivel stools at the counter and old rickety booths that felt like they would collapse under the weight.

The fat waitress came over, threw menus down in front of them and walked away. Ralph picked one up and looked it over. The menu was the strangest thing he'd ever seen - just about half the menu was 'tongue'. Tongue omelets, eggs with tongue and hash browns, tongue sandwiches - it wasn't just the special, it was just about all they had.

The waitress came back over. "What'll ya have?" she asked.

"I'll have the tongue, without so much tongue in it," Ralph said. The waitress stared at him glumly.

"The omelet, please. And a coffee, black," he said handing the menu back to her.

"You stole that from Monty Python," Larry said when she had walked away.

"Who?" Ralph asked.

"The spam thing," Larry replied.

"What are you talking about?" Ralph said, getting irritated.

"Forget it," Larry said.

They ate breakfast in weary silence, then shambled back out to try to find the car again. Ralph barely remembered where the garage was - they circled the block a few times but finally found it. Back at the apartment, Ralph lay down in bed and closed his eyes to try to take a nap, but his whole body was pulsing and throbbing and his eyes kept snapping open again. It looked like he was right, he wasn't going to sleep for awhile.

He crashed all day Saturday and was equally useless on Sunday. He lay around on the couch like a dead fish, trying to watch the ball game but unable to concentrate. Larry called that night.

"You and Pauline call it quits yet?" Ralph asked him.

"Yeah, we're done. Bitch wasn't worth it," Larry said.

"Feel any better?"

"Nope. Still feel like I'm gonna die."

"Yeah, tell that buddy of yours at work to shove it up his ass next time," Ralph said. "I haven't slept since Thursday. Is Frank still alive?"

"No idea, haven't seen him," Larry said.

* * *

Ralph survived another week at work, although he had no idea how. Everyone there was pissing him off and he was ready to start killing them one by one. The Grim Reaper was indeed a nice guy, however - in fact he was almost too nice. Max and Ralph had taken to joking around with him and giving him shit as much as possible, which the Grim Reaper took in stride. Ralph had complained at one point that the Reaper had bad breath, and so Max had come in the next day with a big bottle of Listerine and left it on his desk. The Grim Reaper came out of his office later on to pal around with them.

"That was a good one, guys," he said, laughing good-naturedly.

"No seriously, you should use it though," Ralph said over his shoulder as he typed. "Your breath stinks, man."

"You guys are so funny," the Reaper said, shaking his head and walking away.

***

The band kept practicing at the shithole out past the train tracks, and Ralph was finally able to get some of their stuff down on tape and sent out to a few different places. He hadn't heard anything back yet - however, he had managed to secure them another audition. It was at one of the more popular bars on Hoboken, right off of

Washington Street. Ralph had to lie to get them the audition. Quite a lot, in fact.

He was nervous as hell in the car going over. It was made worse when Larry started to argue with him.

"Why is Frank always sitting in the front seat now?" Larry demanded.

"Because you're an asshole," Ralph grumbled, glaring at him in the rearview mirror.

"No seriously, Frank's always in the front now, when did that change?"

"What kind of happy horseshit is this? Who gives a shit?"

The argument went on. Larry refused to shut up. Every time Ralph looked at him again in the mirror, his blood pressure rose a little bit higher.

"Larry, I swear to God if you don't shut up, I'm gonna kill you," he said. The stars in his eyes were dancing again.

"Go ahead then, your driving is gonna kill us first anyway. By the way, do you even know where the hell you're going? That was the exit, dipshit..."

Someone cut him off in traffic just as Larry finished his latest expulsion. Ralph let go of the wheel and dove headlong into the back seat, lunging at Larry's neck to try to choke him. Larry fought him off and the two started wrestling. From the passenger seat, Frank grabbed ahold of the wheel with one hand, his eyes as wide as saucers as they headed into the trunk of the car in front of them. Frank jerked the wheel, the car veered sharply toward the shoulder and they crashed into the guard rail.

As Ralph extricated himself from the tangle of limbs in the back seat, he pictured what might have been. He saw them lined up three across in a neat little row of hospital beds, all of them wrapped like mummies in full body casts, legs dangling from cables and tubes sticking out of their arms.

"I told you I was gonna kill you," Ralph said as he pulled back onto the highway.

"And I told you about your fuckin' driving. See what you did, now we're gonna be late," Larry said.

They were a mess by the time they got to the bar. Ralph's shirt was soaked through with sweat, and Larry's was almost ripped in half.

"You guys are late," the manager said as they walked in.

"Yeah, we hit some traffic, sorry bout that," Ralph said.

They set their gear up on stage. Larry tripped on the riser and sent the snare drum flying into the toms, causing an unholy racket. Ralph stood off to the side, grinding his teeth. When they were all ready, they started playing. This time they didn't make it through the first song before the whole thing collapsed. Ralph turned around to yell at Larry and the two of them started all over again.

"All right, that's enough," the manager said. They packed the gear right back up and got out of there as quickly as they could.

"He asked us never to come back again. That was a first," Larry quipped from the back seat.

"It's your fault," Ralph said. "You and your mouth."

"Maybe we should have played the blues stuff," Larry said sarcastically.

"Shut the fuck up," Ralph said.

Ralph went to Willy's that night by himself. It was a slow night, no one else was in there. Henry came over to talk.

"I don't know what I'm gonna do," Ralph said over his beer. "Neither one of them can play worth shit, they both suck."

"Then maybe it's time to find other people," the old fellow said. "What are you gonna do? Gotta do what you gotta do."

"Dunno, Henry."

A couple of good-looking girls walked in and sat down at the other end of the bar. Ralph was too tired, he didn't want to bother.

"You hear the Jets got that receiver from Cincinnati? The one that's supposed to be some big deal?" Ralph asked.

"No, hadn't heard. It's the Jets though, it doesn't matter," Henry said.

"One of these days, it's gonna be their year."

"Not in my lifetime."

"C'mon Henry, have a little faith."

"Sorry, all out."

Ralph went home, pulled the shades down, turned all the lights off and sat in the dark with another beer. He listened to the sounds of traffic outside, watched the headlights shine in through the shades. After a while he put some music on the stereo, some old stuff he hadn't heard in a long time. It sounded so good there in the dark - he turned it up louder. Someone started banging on the wall.

"Turn it down!" the guy yelled.

His next-door neighbor was a mechanic with a particularly bad temper who was six foot three and weighed about two hundred fifty pounds. Ralph turned it down.

***

The next morning, the alarm went off.

"Holy shit," Ralph said, spinning around and flinging the pillow into space.

He got up and made coffee, even stronger than usual. It was becoming more and more difficult to wake up in the morning. Off to work he went. The traffic was unthinkably bad, there was no end in sight in any direction. Ralph entertained thoughts of getting out of the car and just leaving it there, getting out and simply walking off in a random direction, come what may. But he didn't do it.

It was eight o' clock at night on Tuesday. Gina had called twice, he hadn't answered. Then someone buzzed the front door. He didn't feel like dealing with anyone's shit that night, and he'd be damned if anyone was going to force him into it. Suddenly he heard banging on the fire escape outside the window.

"I know you're in there bastard, I can see the light on," came a muffled voice from outside. Gina was coming up the ladder.

"Cut the shit Gina, okay, I'm coming down," he said through the closed window. He watched her climb back down again, and then went downstairs to let her in.

"Why don't you ever answer the phone, you shithead," she asked as she sat down.

"Because then I'd have to talk to you," Ralph said, getting a beer.

"Dude - why don't you ever get me one?" she whined at him.

"Get it yourself," he said. She tried to kick him as he collapsed on the couch.

"I got laid the other night," Gina said, smirking to herself and playing with her hair.

"Good for you," Ralph said, trying to ignore her and watch TV. There was a movie on, some oldie about the CIA and Russkie spies or something.

"He wasn't bad looking either. Better looking than you, at least," she said. Ralph glared at her over the top of the beer can.

"Why are you here?" he asked.

"Because I'm bored," Gina said.

"What about the new boyfriend, why don't you go bother him."

"He's not my boyfriend, all I said was I got laid."

"So what's wrong with him?"

"Nothing's wrong with him, shut the fuck up."

Thankfully, there was a lull in the conversation. It lasted about a minute and a half, which was pretty much the limit with Gina.

"You guys are going to Willy's on Friday, right?" she asked.

"Yes," Ralph replied.

"Let me come with you," she said.

"No," he said.

"C'mon Ralph, I'll be good. I won't start any trouble or anything."

"No, Gina."

"Why not?"

"Because you're a pain in the ass."

"C'mon Ralph, don't be an asshole."

Gina worked on him for another few days, calling him constantly to bug the shit out of him about it. Finally he relented, and said she could go with them. Gina let out a little yip of glee over the phone. On Friday night, they all piled into his car and drove over to the bar. Larry tripped on the doorsill again as they went in.

"I'm gonna get you a seeing eye dog," Ralph said to him over his shoulder.

"Ginaaa, how ya doin' there?" asked Henry with a broad smile as they sat down. "Haven't seen you in here in a long time."

"Yeah I know Henry, asshole over here never lets me come, he's too good for me or something," Gina responded. Henry came over with the drinks.

"So what's up Larry?" Gina asked, giving him a friendly slap on the back.

"Nothing Gina, how you doin," Larry said. Larry and Gina had always gotten along pretty well.

"Stayin' outta trouble, you know," she replied. "Got laid the other night."

"Hey, congratulations," Larry said, clinking beer bottles with her. "I know that's a real accomplishment for you."

"Ohhh, fuck you," Gina said laughing.

Ralph was trying to stay out of the whole thing. Having Gina there made him distinctly nervous. He looked around the room at the rather sparse crowd gathered there. The jukebox was playing something mellow and there wasn't a whole lot going on. His eyes came back to rest on Frank as he sat to Gina's left, listening to the conversation. Frank's eyes were glazed over, and he had a dreamy expression on his face as he watched her babble with Larry. For Chrissake - the little fucker had a crush on Gina. He'd never noticed it before.

After awhile, Gina noticed too. She turned to give Frank a big welcoming smile.

"Why can't you guys be gentlemen like your friend Frank over here?" she asked, basking in the attention and fixing him with a big oily come-hither look. Frank beamed. Oh Lord, Ralph thought, fidgeting around. I'm gonna puke if they keep this up.

"Hey, I'm a gentleman too," Larry objected. "I just hide it better than he does."

***

Ralph and Larry were back at Willy's again the next night, this time by themselves.

"Fuckin' Frank has the hots for Gina," Ralph grumbled into his beer.

"Yeah, I know," Larry said matter-of-factly, not bothering to look over.

Ralph eyes widened, he was taken aback. "You *know*?"

"Everybody knows. He was staring at her the entire three months you guys were dating. You're the only one who didn't know."

"Did fuckin' *Gina* know?" Ralph stammered.

"Dunno," Larry said.

Ralph went back to his beer, stewing in his juices. "You gotta be shittin' me," he said after awhile.

"I wouldn't worry about it," Larry said, staring at the TV. "Gina could never go out with someone who doesn't speak. It would drive her crazy."

"Yeah, but she could still fuck him," Ralph said, glowering.

Involuntary visions began dancing in his head. The mere possibility of it was highly disturbing. Nah, Ralph decided after careful internal deliberation. Gina hadn't fucked Frank. She would have said something to him if she had. Her mouth had a mind of its own.

Ralph went home and sat on the floor again, with the shades down and the lights out. He'd been drinking for two days and his head hurt. The next time Gina came up the fire escape, he was going to dump a pot of water on her head.

***

He went back to work on Monday morning. Half the place was sick, there was some sort of Ebola going around. They were running up against a deadline and Ralph sat there all morning, typing away like mad trying to get the work done. Max came by.

"You finished yet? He's asking about it again," Max said.

"No, I'm almost done," Ralph responded, still typing.

"He said they need it by noon at the latest," Max said.

"Well, go in there and tell Darth Vader the Death Star's not in position yet," Ralph said angrily over his shoulder, waving him away.

An hour later, Max came by to check again. Then a few minutes later, the Grim Reaper followed him into the cubicle. The stench of his breath preceded him, it was like a noxious vapor.

"God damn..." Ralph said, screwing up his face and recoiling like he'd just inhaled a skunk.   "Dude, we bought you the Listerine!"

"It's like chemical warfare," Max added.

"Ha ha, I know, that was a good one with the Listerine," said the Reaper, chuckling.

"No, we were actually serious. You're supposed to use it," Max said.

"Look, it's still not ready yet," Ralph said, anticipating the complaint.

"No, I know, never mind about that," the Reaper said. "I came by to introduce you guys to my boss, he's here today and he says he'd like to meet you."

The Boss of Bosses came striding down the aisle. He was a pretty boy, with hair carefully coiffed and pearly teeth gleaming. He wore Georgie O' Marney suits from like eight different countries, and his shoes shone like the sun and the stars. Everything about him was perfect, just the sweat from his earlobe was magnificent.

The Grim Reaper was bent practically in half with unctuous hand-wringing pleasure.

"Ahh, Mr. Wilkinson, may I present two of my finest programmers, Ralph

Sanders and Max Edgar," the Reaper said with a theatrical wave of his hand. The boss confidently strode further forward with great enthusiasm.

"Mike Wilkinson," he said when he'd reached them, shaking their hands vigorously and smiling from ear to ear like a pumpkin. "A real pleasure to meet you."

Mr. Wilkinson's handshake was a thing of beauty, made at the optimal angle and with just the right amount of grip strength. His hands were manicured and his watch was heavy. An exotic fragrance emanated from him, something that smelled properly expensive. His eyebrows were carefully trimmed and his belt buckle glittered like gold. Mike Wilkinson aimed to impress.

"I've heard a whole lot of good things about you fellas," Mr. Wilkinson said, his rictus undiminished as he continued to pump away at Ralph's hand. "You've done some quality work for us, quality work. And I'm fully confident that it will continue well into the future..."

The intensity of Mr. Wilkinson's smile actually increased as he went on, if that were possible. Ralph began to imagine the man's face splitting open at the seams, the flesh pulling away from his skull and liquid magma oozing from the newly-formed fissure. Mr. Wilkinson was so successful, it almost appeared life-threatening.

"Well, I'm afraid I've got to be going. A real pleasure to have met you both," Mr. Wilkinson said. He gave the Grim Reaper a winning smile of his own, turned on his heel and marched back up the aisle.

"That was quite an opportunity for you," the Reaper said once he'd gone. "Mr. Wilkinson doesn't visit here often."

"My life has been changed forever," Max said with a skeptical raised eyebrow. "Nothing will ever be the same."

The Reaper laughed. "Ha ha, you guys are too much, I'll tell you that."

Ralph was too demoralized to comment, to respond or to move. Eventually, he trudged back into his cube and sat down, praying for death, or at least that they'd all go away. And his wish was granted - but not for long. Udarsh came calling shortly after lunch.

"So, I came over to get a status on that module you've been writing, the one that was due last week," Udarsh said sourly.

"Oh, don't you start," Ralph said, disgusted. "Max," he called over the cube wall, "can you come over here, I'm gonna need a translation again."

"I can't believe you have to do this each and every time - why can't you just give me a simple answer for once?" Udarsh was instantly irate, his upper lip quivering as he stood with his hands on his hips.

Ralph sat there gaping at him, shaking his head dismissively.

"Unbelievable," he said. "I don't know how you function. I mean, how do you order takeout? What if someone calls you on the phone when you're at home?"

Udarsh stared back, grinding his teeth and getting more frustrated by the second.

"I know damn well you know what I'm saying you son of a bitch, everyone else can understand me just fine, I told you about a thousand times already."

Max came over to sort things out, and Ralph was soon left in peace once more. The rest of the day lasted about a week. When he got home that night Ralph had a throbbing headache, so he drank about eight beers and tried to go to sleep. That place was going to kill him, it was only a matter of time.

He lay there in bed, imagining what it would be like to wrap his fingers slowly around Udarsh's neck and just squeeze. He'd squeeze for about three days; he'd squeeze until they pulled him off and the cops came to get him. Then he pictured himself sitting despondently with the other inmates in some jail cell, waiting for Larry to come and bail him out. He continued to be amazed that he'd yet to see the inside of one.

* * *

They went to Hoboken on Friday night. It was six o' clock and they were sitting at a table eating pizza at a place on Washington Street, just screwing around until it was time to drink. 'The Girl From Ipanema' came on the radio.

"That's like some fancy Mexican shit or something, what is that?" Larry asked after listening to it for a while.

"'The Girl From Ipanema'," Ralph said with his mouth full.

"Hmm, never heard it before."

"You grew up under a rock."

They finished eating and went down the street.

"You never heard that song before, admit it," Ralph chided Larry as he walked a few steps behind him.

Ralph continued, "Dude, it's like the most famous song ever made. They play it on the light FM stations about once an hour, in the elevators and everything."

"Light FM my ass," Larry laughed, mocking him. "I've never heard that song before in my life, and they weren't even singing in English..."

"Yes they were too fucking singing in English, were you even listening to it??" Ralph spat, immediately tense.

"You're so full of shit - Frank, have you ever heard that song before?" Frank shrugged his shoulders, he wasn't sure.

Ralph was growling audibly. He was friends with two of the greatest nitwits of all time. Larry was still making noise behind him, droning on and on about absolutely nothing. In his mind's eye, Ralph pictured himself suddenly producing a megaphone, spinning around and screaming *'SHUT THE FUCK UP!'* at him in a gravelly megaphone

Satan voice. It would feel so satisfying to do it, just once.

"Larry, I'm going to hit you," he informed him instead.

"Go ahead, tough guy."

They stopped in at one of the trendy bars along the way. Ralph had been horny for weeks now, he had to get laid soon. But it was too early, the birds were all still in their nests. A beer would have to do for now.

They stayed in Hoboken until past midnight. No one hooked up or got laid - they stood around drinking beer and having a generally miserable time. The kids got younger and younger, and Ralph got older and older. He was starting to feel like someone's father or something. Past ten o' clock or so and the bartenders now looked at him like he should be somewhere else. What did you do when you were old and wanted to have fun? The prospects didn't look promising.

***

The following day was his mother's birthday. He had to call, there was no choice. He picked up the phone and dialed.

"Hello?" his mother said.

"Happy birthday, Ma," Ralph said.

"Well it's *about time*!" she shrieked. "Why haven't you called???" He hung up.

***

Gina came over. She threw herself down on the couch and sprawled out with her legs up. Gina sat uncharacteristically quiet for a moment, then dropped her big bombshell: she was now dating the guy she'd had sex with a few weeks earlier.

"Don't worry, it won't last," Ralph said.

"You know, I think your friend Frank likes me. He was giving me the eyes that night at the bar," she said, crossing her legs and bouncing her foot around. Ralph looked over and saw an impish little smirk crawling across her face.

"Gina, do me a favor and don't have sex with Frank - he's got enough problems already," he said.

"Maybe I'll do it just to piss you off," she said, still grinning.

"Lovely," he said under his breath.

"I'm hungry. Let's order some Chinese," Gina said.

"I hate Chinese food, you know that." Ralph said.

"C'mon, it's good every once in a while," she insisted. "We haven't had it in a long time."

He gave in, and they called the Chinese place down the street to have some food sent over. Ralph refrained from making any wise cracks over the phone about whether the 'Dog in Cat Sauce' special was any good that day. The delivery guy came and they tucked in, eating in relative silence. The only time Gina was ever quiet was when she was eating.

***

Now it was Friday night and Ralph needed a chick, bad. It was either find one tonight or die. They jumped on the train and headed into the city to do some bar hopping, first stop Roscoes as usual. Ralph was amped up, too much so: the nervous energy was coursing through him like lightning. His limbs were twitching a bit and he was afraid he was going to lash out involuntarily and smack someone by accident. A girl was standing next to him. She was pretty damn ugly but he was desperate.

"Buy you a drink?" he asked, trying to smile.

"I'm with someone," she said, pointing backward at some guy standing behind them.

Ralph downed his beer and chased it with another. Larry tried to talk to him but he ignored him - there was only one thing on his mind. A second girl showed up next to him, trying to get the bartender's attention.

"Buy you a drink?" he tried again. This one ignored him completely, in fact she looked downright offended.

God damn it," Ralph said. He had another beer. Larry came over again.

"Let's go to another place," Ralph suggested.

Larry agreed, they grabbed Frank and left. They walked through the Village trying a few different spots along the way, but no luck. It just wasn't Ralph's night. In fact it wasn't his week, or his year, or his lifetime for that matter. He was fucked, there was no other way to look at it.

They were at the last place, it was getting near closing time and Ralph was good and drunk by now. It was some upscale nightclub type of deal that Larry said would have chicks in it. People were hooking up left and right all around them and Ralph was getting pissed off. In fact, he'd been pissed off for hours now.

"It's getting late, they're gonna close soon," Larry said.

"Yeah I know," Ralph said.

"This place sucks."

"I know that too. It was your idea."

"Frank's drunk."

Ralph didn't reply. He didn't care if Frank was drunk or not. Larry looked around the room in a dull stupor.

"We should be getting back, it's almost last call," he said.

"**CRACK BABY**!!! I know that!!" Ralph exploded. The music was loud enough to mask the outburst for the most part, but the fashionable group standing next to them shot Ralph a quartet of dirty looks.

Last call came and went, and they got out of there. Outside on the sidewalk, Larry was all bent out of shape.

You know, you have emotional problems, are you aware of that?"

"Only when someone repeats the same thing ten fucking times. You're like a broken record," Ralph said.

"You're just pissed because you can't find anyone stupid enough to hook up with you," Larry said.

"Well at least I'm trying, you assfuck," Ralph said. "You sit there the whole time, you don't do anything. You must be some kinda fag or something."

"You're the one that takes it up the ass," Larry countered.

Ralph turned around and shoved him, and the two of them started wrestling in the street. "Stupid fucking faggot," Ralph seethed between grunts, trying to get Larry in a headlock. They tripped on the curb and went over in a drunken heap. Ralph got up on unsteady legs, staring wildly at Larry.

"You pole-smoking pickle-shining fart-knocking dick-licking... ass bandit... *butt pirate*!!!" he screamed uncontrollably.

Larry went to respond, but the comprehensive genius of it stopped the argument in its tracks. There was no response to that. They brushed themselves off, and then the three of them went up the street stumbling like hoboes toward the train station. They were now firmly in danger of missing the last train.

The hangover from hell arrived the next morning. Ralph veered into walls as he held the contents of his head in place between his hands and tried to find the shower. He moaned his way through a cup of coffee, thought about opening the blinds and decided against it. The light might finish him off. Larry called on the phone.

"I'm quitting the band," he announced.

"You are not," Ralph replied, and hung up.

They went out again the following weekend. It was another fancy bar in the city where the chicks were supposed to be congregating. Ralph was still in heat but he had all but given up. He sat there glumly nursing his drink while the social whirlwind spun round.

"Doubt we're gonna have much luck in here," Larry said, scanning the joint. "These chicks are pretty full of themselves."

"It's not just here," Ralph replied. "They're bitches everywhere."

"Can't say I disagree," Larry said, taking a sip of his beer. "Almost makes you wish you were gay. Wouldn't have to worry about them then."

"Speak for yourself. See, I knew you took it up the ass," Ralph said.

"No, but you know what I'm saying. It's just too much of a headache."

"You said it."

They clinked glasses and drank to the consensus they'd reached. Ralph looked around the room, loathing the fairer sex a little more with every head of long blonde hair that came into view, every tight little ass that shook in his direction.

One of the tarts came up to the bar, long and lithe and dressed to kill, fixing Ralph with the old get back stare as she prepared to order another drink. He eyeballed her back for a change. She shot him one more glance full of self-important malice before turning around to strike a sultry pose for the benefit of the fellow in the suit who'd come to stand guard over her. He imagined what it would be like to rear back and punch her in the face so hard that she flew clear across the bar and went smashing into the huge mirror hanging behind the rows of expensive liquor bottles. But that would most certainly land him in all sorts of trouble. He'd been to jail about ten times in his head already - he and the inmates were the best of friends by now, they'd all line up to say goodbye to him as he walked out of the cell to go post bail.

There was nothing to be done, it was all a mess. Ralph went home and lay awake in bed all night long, staring at the ceiling and listening to the ticking of the clock. No chick, a job he couldn't stand, a couple of knuckleheads for friends and a whole lotta nothing to do, that was his life. What was the point? Cheerios in the morning, beer at night, baseball games and TV dinners, bills to pay and taxes and then death as your reward. If this was the extent of the human experience, then humanity could stick its head up its own ass.

Ralph went to the drive-thru at McDonalds for lunch. There was either something wrong with the intercom or the girl working there was an insect, all it did was buzz at him.

"I can't understand you," Ralph said.

The buzzing repeated itself. Ralph leaned closer to the box.

"I still can't hear you."

The noise came back louder now, the hornets were becoming angry.

"I'll drive around," Ralph said.

He pulled the car up to the window. The girl sitting there was fat and looked disgruntled.

"You guys need to fix that thing," Ralph said. She sat there, chewing her gum and staring at him like a frog.

"No seriously, it's just a whole lotta noise," he said. He placed his order with a sigh.

"That'll be $5.24", the girl said, ignoring the complaint. Ralph handed her the money. She turned around and waddled off to go look for his food.

Back at the apartment, Ralph sat mulling over why most experiences in life seemed to have become uncomfortable lately. Whether you were driving down the street or going shopping at the supermarket or just ordering a burger at the goddamn drive-thru window, something inevitably happened to wreck your day. Either the world had gone mad, or he had. What was there to do, he was stuck with it either way he supposed.

In the afternoon Ralph was bored. He is called Gina.

"Come on, let's go see a movie."

"Oh, what, you're not too good for me all of a sudden?" she asked mockingly. "The big man calls me on the phone. I guess I'm supposed to feel honored or something."

"Cut the crap, you wanna go or not?"

"Okay fine. What do you wanna see, what's playing?"

They went and saw a movie then drove back home. It was Sunday night; the weekend was over yet again. One of these days he was going to jump out a window when that fucking alarm went off in the morning.

* * *

The week was pure hell. They had a huge demo coming up soon that they were nowhere near ready for. Ralph and Max typed away like crazy in their little boxes, the Grim Reaper came by periodically to breathe down their necks, Ralph fought the Indian off whenever necessary and after an eternity it was Friday again. Ralph sat in his car on the way home, the traffic was snarled and going nowhere fast. It seemed like it was getting worse over time, and he was seriously entertaining thoughts of moving to Wyoming.

Larry was over at the apartment that night.

"I'm moving to Wyoming," Ralph told him.

"Now *there's* a good idea," Larry said, snickering.

"No, I've had it with this shit. Fucking place sucks, all I do is sit in traffic."

"And Wyoming is going to be an improvement?"

"The way I feel right now, anything would be."

"Look, you'd get all the way out there, look at all the nice wide open space and the mountains and clouds and all the cows and things, home on the range and all that bullshit, then you'd wake up the next morning and the first thing you'd say is 'what the fuck am I doing in Wyoming?'. Trust me on this. I know a guy who tried it, actually. A dude I used to work with, got hung up on some chick big time and moved out to Idaho to go live out there with her. He lasted like three months and then he came right back," Larry said, going for another beer.

Ralph considered it for a moment. "Yeah, you're right," he conceded. "Fuck."

Larry came back in, sat down and turned on the TV.

"What about the south?" Ralph suggested. "At least it's closer."

"Buncha rednecks," Larry replied. "NASCAR and shit. They sit there and watch cars going in circles for like four hours. Literally four hours."

"They got hockey in some of those places now, you know."

"Yeah, but they don't watch it. It's third world down there."

***

The next morning they went to the beach. It was Labor Day weekend at the Jersey Shore, and everyone was out for the final fling of the summer. It was a nice day; the sun was shining and the boardwalk was packed. The three of them meandered through the crowd, parting the seas of tough guys with girlfriends and parents toting kids wearing water wings and eating cotton candy.

"Look at this fuckin' guy," Larry said under his breath as they passed a brawny fellow clutching his girl possessively by the waist. "His arms are bigger than his head." He was a big Italian dude who was strutting down the boardwalk puffing his hairy chest out as his gut hung over his goofy bathing suit. His girlfriend was about half his size.

"What's the point of getting that big?" Ralph wondered out loud.

"Gets you laid, I guess," Larry said.

They stopped along the way to get a hot dog and a beer.

"You're wearing those sunglasses again. I thought you said you couldn't see anything in them," Ralph said.

"I can't. But I like 'em anyway," Larry said, munching on his food.

"You're a genius, you know that?"

"Hey Frank, you gonna go in the water this time?"

Frank frowned, gave it a think and shook his head no. Frank didn't like the water; they'd only ever seen him go in one time.

They stood at the counter watching the people go back and forth. Larry's attention was drawn to a young schoolgirl who was talking with her friends. His head swiveled as she went by.

"Get ahold of yourself," Ralph murmured. "Quit with the jailbait."

"I'll betcha that chick was pretty close to eighteen."

"Whadd're you, stupid or what? She's about twelve. Besides, close doesn't count, you moron. It's one or the other, you're either fucked or you're not."

"Yeah, like you didn't look."

They finished their snack and headed toward the water to go swim for a while and relax. The sun was directly overhead and it was getting hot. Kids ran by kicking sand, pretty girls sauntered past down by the water's edge. The wind picked up and started blowing umbrellas around.

"Let's get outta here, I hate the beach," Larry groused.

"You hate the beach, you hate Great Adventure, you hate everything," Ralph said.

"That's not true - I love you," Larry said sarcastically, flashing him a prissy smile.

"So why do you hate the beach?"

"The sand, the salt water, everything sticks to you, the crowds, it's too fuckin' hot, there's no shade. Gimme a nice lake any day of the week. Or air-conditioning."

"Frank, what do you think? You sick of it yet, you wanna go back?" Frank shrugged.

They stuck it out for another half hour, then toweled off and headed for the boardwalk. On the way back to the car, they passed an arcade place that had some kind of ring-tossing game out front.

"Come on, I want to win something for my Mom," Larry said. They went over.

"Three throws for a dollar, you land on any of the red cones and you get a prize," the kid said. He was a skinny kid who looked bored out of his mind.

"I'm good at this," Larry said, stepping up to the plate.

They took turns tossing the rings and no one hit a damn thing. The cones were almost the same size as the rings, there was practically no chance of landing one. It was a rigged game.

"This shit isn't regulation," Ralph said. The kid scoffed.

They tried about five times, then Larry got mad and started cursing. A few more tries and he was firing rings around in frustration.

"Hey, what the hell's wrong with you guys? It's just a game," the kid said in disbelief.

"No, that's bullshit, I want my money back," Larry said.

"No refunds, it's right there on the sign," the kid responded, pointing at it.

"Okay how 'bout I wrap this ring around that little pencil neck of yours then, ya fuckin' geek?" Larry fumed, making it like he was about to reach over the counter.

"Get outta here," the kid laughed. "You guys are crazy, go get a life."

They walked away still pissing and moaning. The sun was dropping lower in the sky, it was time to go back. The Parkway was a sea of cars and Ralph wondered if they would ever make it home.

"This is what I'm talking about," he said as they sat there idling. "Wyoming, I'm tellin' ya."

***

The nights were getting colder. Fall hadn't arrived yet, but it was in the mail.

Ralph decided to quit with the bars for a little while. He was tired of being hungover all the time, and his liver was starting to hurt. He felt bad for it. And anyways, he figured it would be a good way of saving some money for a change - about half his income seemed to be going for beer nowadays.

The band continued practicing and going steadily nowhere. Ralph had been unable to procure any further auditions, and his frustrations continued to mount. Neither of his fellow bandmates ever seemed to improve, not even accidentally. Larry's tempo was all over the place, he switched gears as often as a race-car driver - Ralph felt like he spent the whole time just chasing the beat, to the exclusion of all else. And Frank got so lost sometimes, he would stop playing entirely and just watch the proceedings. They were all getting older by the minute, and the window of opportunity was closing fast. If their big break didn't come soon, Ralph was going to have to start robbing banks. The cash was just sitting there in nice tidy bags on the other side of the wall, all he had to do was go in there and get it. All he knew was that he was not about to spend the rest of his life sitting in a cubicle being accosted by subnormals. Failure was not an option.

They went out drinking on the weekend, there was nothing else to do. They'd gone into Hoboken again for a change of scenery and were sitting at the bar with their beers in front of them. The mood was mellow, almost desultory. A few other early birds were wandering around the place but it was empty for the most part.

A girl came in and sat down on the stool next to Ralph. She was dark-haired with a few too many pounds on her, but still attractive enough. Ralph was in no mood for games, he stared straight ahead and ignored her.

"So how's your day going?" she asked him out of the blue.

He turned, caught off guard. "Not too bad," he said.

"My name's Patty," she said, holding out her hand. How odd. Ralph shook it.

"You come in here often?" she asked him. That was supposed to be his line.

"Not really. We don't go to Hoboken too much."

"Why ya here tonight?"

"That's a good question," he said with a smirk. He was waiting for her to get tired of it and walk off, but she didn't. Instead she ordered a beer.

"So Patty, you live around here?" Ralph asked.

"Yep. Just a few blocks away actually, over on 8th Street."

"You like it here?"

"It's okay, I guess. The people kinda suck but there's a lot to do."

"Agreed," he said, taking a sip of beer.

As they chatted he began to inspect her a bit, looking her up and down and wondering what could be wrong with her. I mean this didn't happen, chicks didn't just come up to you and start talking. Something had to be amiss. But try as he might, he couldn't spot anything terribly out of place. She was animated, a little frenetic even, but nothing to get in a twist over.

The night wore on and Patty stuck around; in fact, she wouldn't leave his side. Ralph was drinking the beers down too fast and things were getting blurry. Larry came over for a status check.

"Fuck off, I'm getting laid," Ralph said under his breath.

"It's about time," Larry said, and went back to his stool.

"He's getting laid," he informed Frank as he sat down. Frank flashed the thumbs-up sign.

By ten o' clock, the bar was hopping and Ralph was drunk. Patty had had quite a few herself, she looked tipsy but she was hanging in there. She leaned over to whisper something sultry in Ralph's ear.

"Let's go back to my place," she cooed, giving his earlobe a love bite as she said it.

Ralph tabbed out, gave Larry and Frank a pointed look as he passed and went out the door to follow Patty up the street. She was jovial and laughing, dancing around in front of him on the sidewalk as they went, much to the stern annoyance of the oncoming yuppies. They got to her building and went inside.

"Ohhh, I'm so high on life I could just scream!" she screamed as she threw her keys on the table. She pirouetted over to the stereo and turned on some music.

Ralph sat down on the couch. "Nice place," he said. "Got any beer?"

"Yeah, it's not much but it's home," Patty said, going into the kitchen and returning with a can of beer. Ralph cracked it open and drank deeply. A catchy song came on and Patty shrieked once again.

"I love this song, it's absolutely my favorite!" She started singing along excitedly, squealing in a high-pitched off-key voice loudly enough that Ralph started listening for the inevitable sound of pounding on the other side of the wall. But the pounding never came - maybe they were all still out at the bars.

Ralph finished his beer, the song ended and another came on. Patty loved this one even more than the first and resumed her performance, the singing now accompanied by a gyrating interpretive dance of some sort. Patty was really letting loose; the noise was almost deafening. Her eyes were closed, her brow furrowed in fervent concentration as she sung away with abandon. Ralph was starting to see the light. Here was the punch line he'd been waiting for all night long.

Suddenly she dove on top of him as he sprawled on the couch, clawing at him desperately as she kissed him.

"Take me inside and make love to me!" she said. "You've conquered me, I'm powerless to resist, I don't care anymore!"

"Are you feeling all right?" Ralph said tentatively, once he'd extracted his lower lip from her mouth.

"Yeah, why?" she asked, sitting up for a moment. "Oh, am I acting a little crazy? I ran out of meds yesterday actually, I never got over to the pharmacy like I was supposed to," she replied.

"You ran out of meds?" he repeated, eyes widening in disbelief.

"Yeah, I'm on this stuff that's supposed to keep me calm, even out my moods and all that. But I'm feeling wonderful right now! I'm on top of the world!!" Patty ripped her shirt off and threw it on the floor. "Take me into the bedroom and ravish me..." she insisted, scratching at him and growling like a tiger.

Ralph did a quick calculation in his head, weighed discretion against valor and quickly opted for the latter. 'Fuck it - if she stabs me in my sleep, at least I'll die happy,' he said to himself as he picked her up and carried her into the other room. Ralph laid the girl down on the bed and stripped off his clothes as she dispensed with what remained of her own. He went to lay down next to her but she immediately grabbed him by the shoulders, pinning him down on the bed and sitting on top of him.

"I wanna be on top..." Patty said, laughing, a wild look dancing in her eyes. Ralph began to wonder if he'd passed the point of no return or if there was still a chance to flee. They started pumping away and now Patty was singing again, as loudly as before or even louder. Still no pounding on the walls.

They bumped and grinded and Patty just kept going - she was insatiable, like some elemental phenomenon, an unstoppable force of nature. Ralph had become exhausted but there was no stopping her. Finally he bucked her off and gently moved her to the side.

"Honey, I got nothin' left," he said, breathing heavily and wiping the sweat off his forehead.

"What's the matter? Don't you love me?" she asked. Her lower lip was beginning to tremble. Oh shit. Where were the kitchen knives?

"No, I'm just tired is all," he said.

"You don't love me, do you? Just admit it, you don't love me! You were using me all along!" Patty whined as she began to cry.

"No, look, you're great but we only just met, and I don't know - "

"*Tell me you love me!*" she commanded sternly, her face suddenly growing hard.

"Okay, okay, I love you," he said.

"No you don't! I don't believe you!!" She threw herself down face-first into the pillow, sobbing in despair.

"Shit," Ralph said, getting up to find his clothes.

"Get out!!" Patty screeched suddenly. "I don't ever want to see you again!" She picked up the lamp on the end table and flung it at his head. He ducked and it smashed into the wall behind him.

Ralph dove to the floor, reaching around to collect his clothes and shoes before she could reload. He gathered them up in a ball and stood up to find her wielding a chair.

"I'm sick of you bastards doing this," she snarled. "You're gonna pay this time, you motherfucker." She lunged forward. Ralph sprinted into the living room and made it out of there just in time, slamming the door to the sound of crunching wood following close behind.

***

Larry called the next day. "So how'd it go there, loverboy?"

"Holy shit, she was a psycho. Completely loony tunes. Off her meds. Literally," Ralph said.

"Well what did you expect? She went home with you, didn't she?" Larry said.

"Shut the fuck up," Ralph said.

"So she made Gina look sane, eh?"

"You have no idea. I barely escaped with my life."

"Meh. There are worse ways to go. So, won't be seeing her again?"

"No. She threw a chair at me."

Ralph was rummaging around in the cushions as they talked, trying to find the clicker - the Mets game was coming on.

"We gotta practice this week," he said to Larry absentmindedly.

"Dude, you need to give it up, once and for all," Larry said. "We ain't goin' anywhere, face it."

"You know what your problem is? Your fuckin' mental attitude, that's what. You guys are losers because you can't imagine winning. That's the problem with this fuckin' band," Ralph fumed, immediately seeing red.

"No, the problem with this band is that no one in it can play music," Larry retorted. Ralph slammed the phone down, then pulled the cord clear out of the wall.

***

The big demo at work was all set for the following day, and the fires were blazing furiously as Ralph and Max fought to get everything in place. There was a meeting in the conference room with all the developers, a little pow-wow to iron out all the final details. One of them was another Indian guy whose accent closely resembled Udarsh's. Every time he spoke, Ralph made a big show of understanding him perfectly, flashing Udarsh a wide devilish grin every time he did so. Udarsh sat there muttering to himself. The Grim Reaper went to the front of the room.

"Look guys, I know it's been a long hard slog but we're almost there. Let's get all our ducks in a row and finalize everything as soon as possible, so that we can really nail this thing tomorrow."

Ralph and Max exchanged a look - the Reaper enjoyed his pep talks a little too much.

"We're looking forward to giving our very best effort, boss," Max piped up.

"Thank you, Max," the Reaper said, beaming happily and missing the sarcasm completely.

Udarsh was about to give a status report to the team and he came over to check something with Ralph first, looking positively horrified in advance. Ralph was shaking his head sadly before Udarsh had even started.

"What is he trying to say?" he asked Max, who was sitting on his other side.

"Such a motherfucker, I can't stand it," Udarsh seethed under his breath, trying to keep his voice down so the others wouldn't hear.

"He wants us to run a few more tests on that second module," Max informed him.

"Then why didn't he tell us that?" Ralph said.

"Motherfucker," Udarsh said.

Ralph went back to his cubicle and did nothing for a long time. He hated giving presentations, they were pure torture - all those horrible beady eyes bearing down on him, just waiting for him to slip up or say the wrong thing. It felt like being slowly boiled in oil. He began to pray that an earthquake or some other such act of god might come along within the next few hours to demolish the building, or at least render the conference room unusable for a while. Maybe a lightning strike. Preferably one centered on Udarsh's cube.

Max came over to lean casually against the wall of the cube. "All set?" he asked, munching on a pretzel.

I guess. Really don't want to do this thing tomorrow though."

"No shit, neither do I. Let's just get it over with then."

"Who's gonna do the talking?"

"We all are, we're gonna take turns. Udarsh says he wants to do his part at the end, so you and I'll go first."
"Lovely."

***

Ralph went home and threw some leftovers in the microwave for dinner. The answering machine's light was off, no one had called. The burly mechanic next door was having a screaming match with his wife, he heard crashing and things being thrown around. After a while it died down and silence settled in again. He had told himself no beer tonight, but the thought of having to do this fucking demo tomorrow was just about melting his brain, it wouldn't leave him alone. Ralph went to the fridge and got a beer, finished it off in five minutes and went for another. He had a feeling it wasn't going to stop there either. Shit.

He passed out around midnight, then woke up again at two, turned over on his back and lay awake for the rest of the night. In the morning he dragged his hangover into the kitchen to make coffee, feeling like a condemned man about to be led to the gallows. Maybe he'd just quit, call up and say 'see ya later': he didn't see why not, he couldn't stand the job anyway. He pissed and moaned for a while then reluctantly decided quitting probably wasn't the wisest course of action to take - otherwise it was back to school buses and kids' birthday parties and he didn't know if he'd be able to handle that. Instead he would just go in there, say as little as humanly possible and let Max do most of the heavy lifting. Max loved to talk anyway; he wouldn't mind.

He went in and they were in the conference room already.   Udarsh was pacing off to the side, he looked extremely agitated. Ralph ignored him and went to help Max set up the computer. The Grim Reaper was busy playing with the projector, looking perplexed.

The crowd shuffled in and took their seats - there were a lot of people there, more than he'd expected. Ralph started to sweat. Max led off, breezing through his material as if without a care in the world. Public speaking never seemed to bother him for some reason. Once Max had wrapped up, Ralph launched into his spiel. He ran the program in the background as he addressed the group, and then wouldn't you know it the thing started to seize up, the network issues were back again. He felt his blood beginning to rise, as the sweat ran down from under his arms and soaked his shirt with nasty blotches. Ralph gritted his teeth as he forced himself to make apologies for the technical difficulties and tried to rush through the rest of the presentation.

Udarsh was impatient and began to chime in as Ralph neared the finish line. There was only a little bit left and he was anxious to be done with it, but his little Indian nemesis just wouldn't let him finish. Ralph didn't know what Udarsh was saying, all he knew was that Udarsh was now talking over him every time he went to speak. Ralph started to breathe heavily, trying in vain to control himself. Udarsh shot him an evil, smirking glance as he continued babbling: it was payback time.

Faulty circuits started firing in Ralph's head, the stars were flashing and alarms were going off and Udarsh just would not stop talking. The starbursts flared away, now a dazzling fireworks display ricocheting around inside his skull. This was it; the time had come.   Unceremoniously picking up the keyboard and brandishing it from one end, he turned and bashed Udarsh in the face with it as hard as he could, dropping him like a sack of potatoes. The impact made a rattling crack, to the mortification of all those present. The police arrived shortly thereafter.

***

Larry came down to bail him out, and then they drove back in the car.

"So you finally made it to jail - just like you said you would," Larry quipped. "How was it?"

"Pretty boring, actually," Ralph said.

"You get fucked in the ass?" Larry asked.

"No but I've got a date next week," Ralph said. "I'm hungry, you want some Taco Bell?"

They pulled into the drive-thru, ate some burritos in the car and then Ralph went home. There was a message on the machine telling Ralph he'd been fired. Not exactly surprising.

His court date had been scheduled for early the following month. Ralph pled guilty to smashing someone in the face with a keyboard, and since it was his first offense he got off with a suspended sentence, a fine and a little bit of community service. Autumn drifted by and soon they were into October. Ralph spent his time moping around the apartment doing nothing. Then one day he got a letter in the mail.

"We got a gig," he told Larry.

"A what?"

"A gig, a show."

"Where?"

"It's in Denmark."

There was a long pause. "Are you on drugs?" Larry asked.

"No, I'm serious. They responded to one of the CDs I sent out. They want us to go over there and play a gig. It's part of some festival or something."

"Why the fuck would they want that?"

"They said we sound like some punk band that's popular over there right now. They're gonna buy us plane tickets and everything, put us up in a hotel, the whole nine yards. It's at the end of the month."

"You gotta be shittin' me. But we suck."

Ralph was getting mad, but he restrained himself. "You want me to tell them that? 'Sorry we can't play, because we suck'?"

"It's in Denmark? What the fuck's in Denmark?"

"The Danish, I guess."

"The pastries?"

"No, the people."

"Are we getting paid?"

"Yeah, but it's not much. What the hell does that matter, it's a gig isn't it? We've been looking for one for like a year and now you want to bitch about the money?"

There was another lengthy pause as Larry tried to process the information. "We're gonna fly over to Denmark. Okay sure, why not."

Later in the day they went and told Frank, who rather predictably didn't have much to say about it. Ralph called the contact from the letter and told him they'd do it. The deal was finalized on the phone, and the plane tickets arrived in the mail a few days later.

"Okay we've gotta practice like there's no tomorrow now," Ralph told them.

"Yeah, that's easy for someone who has no job," Larry fired back.

"Don't be an asshole. This is the real deal, an actual paying gig. One that's going to be seen by actual people. I'm not gonna fall on my face again, we're gonna do this right for once for Chrissake. You guys need to get your asses in gear."

So for three solid weeks they practiced every day, going down to the abandoned building across the railroad tracks and hitting it as hard as they could. In the beginning it was the same old shit, but as the days progressed they pulled it together enough so that at least they could finish songs without crashing and burning. By the time they were ready to get on board the plane, they sounded downright competent - damn good in fact, Ralph thought. Even Larry wasn't griping about how bad they were anymore. The beats were consistent, the bass and guitar were in sync, everything was shipshape and all squared away. This was it, Ralph could feel it. The big time, at last.

***

The flight was out of Newark. They drove over in Ralph's car, put it down in the economy lot, dropped the bags and gear off and went through security. Larry's drums were taped up haphazardly in old cardboard boxes he'd found lying around in his parents' garage.

"That shit will never survive the trip," Ralph observed. "You're gonna be banging on garbage cans for the gig." 'And it won't sound any different', he added to himself.

They got beers at the gate and waited, then it was time to board. Ralph hadn't been on a plane since he was a little kid and his stomach was turning over in knots. Larry didn't look terribly happy about it either. Frank looked like he always did, nothing ever bothered him.

They were seated three across in the middle section, with Ralph at the end and Larry between them. The flight was relatively smooth and they didn't hit too much turbulence. They got more beers from the stewardess and tried to relax. About halfway through the flight, the meal service started and they ate some dinner.

Frank finished eating and slouched down in his seat to take a nap. Ralph and

Larry had put down a few more beers and were getting restless. Larry began poking Ralph in the ribs repeatedly to try to get a rise out of him. Ralph poked back. The poking contest continued, Ralph jabbed harder then punched Larry in the thigh, prompting an 'oof'. Larry reached over to push the button for Ralph's overhead light, and Ralph returned the favor. The couple in the aisle seats next to them were now watching. Larry picked up his dinner roll and plunked it in Ralph's cup of soda, which prompted in return a shower of salad dressing all over his tray. Larry reached for Ralph's buttons again and caught a glancing elbow to the jaw, prompting a short yelp of surprise. Larry fended off the attack with his own upraised elbow and managed to hit Ralph's flight attendant call button.

Ralph was getting mad. He took his soda and flung it in Larry's face, missing partially and spraying Frank as he lay sleeping. The people in front of them were starting to turn around in their seats to object. Larry picked up a handful of food to throw and so Ralph took his coffee and dumped it in Larry's lap. Larry howled in pain and took an awkward swing at Ralph's head.

Ralph grunted and swung back. One of Larry's fingers caught him in the eye and Ralph screamed - he swung again, then lunged forward to wrap his hands around Larry's neck and strangle him.

Two stewardesses came striding quickly down the aisle. The first one reached over to turn the call light off, while the other stood there with her hands on her hips, glaring at them.

"All right, what is going on here?" she demanded.

Ralph and Larry stopped what they were doing and turned to face her, looking up simultaneously like synchronized Japanese tourists. There was a standoff as the two sides stared at each other in silence.

"Are the two of you finished?" the stewardess finally asked. Ralph nodded yes like a penitent schoolboy. The two women marched angrily back up the aisle.

"Your fault," Ralph said.

"Was not, you started it," Larry countered.

"I'm gonna kill you before we get to Denmark," Ralph said.

"Asshat," Larry said. Frank was still asleep.

They got off the plane groggy as hell from the red-eye flight and took a taxi to the hotel. It was a modest little place on the outskirts of town that their sponsors had reserved for them. Ralph was exhausted and immediately took a nap, while the other two went for a walk to check out the neighborhood a bit. They came back around lunchtime.

"Goddamn Danish, some Heidi chick was yodeling something at me on the street," Larry said as he came in through the door, with Frank trailing close behind.

"You know the Danes aren't the Swiss, right?" Ralph said sardonically as he rubbed the sleep from his eyes.

"What do you mean?" Larry asked.

"They don't yodel here. They yodel in Switzerland."

"Nah, it's all chocolate and watches and lederhosen and shit over here, it's all the same."

"None of those things are Danish, you dipshit."

"Whadd're you, the King of Greenland?"

"The hell does that mean?"

"Never mind, don't worry about it."

Ralph went into the bedroom to get his electric razor. "You know they got these things in France called bidets, they shoot water up your ass after you go to the bathroom," he said as he came out.

"Get the fuck outta here, they do not," Larry scoffed. "You're making that shit up."

"No I swear to God, they do. I saw it on one of those travel specials on TV," Ralph said from the bathroom. "Fuckin' bunch of weirdos."

After lunch, they went out to explore Copenhagen. It was only midway through the Fall, but it was cold and windy there already. The streets were lined with big stately buildings, very neat and orderly and overly sane. And everything was crazy expensive, the whole place smelled of money. Just about everyone there spoke English and the girls were all cute as hell. The three of them were in heat - Frank in particular, who was walking down the street with his tongue hanging out.

They went down to the water to check out the Little Mermaid. The people at the hotel had been telling them about it, it was supposed to be some sort of must-see attraction, a statue poking its head out of the sea or something. It was small, extremely small.

"That's it? That's their fuckin' monument?" Larry said.

"Not exactly the Eiffel Tower, is it," Ralph agreed dryly, looking down at it as he leaned over the railing.

"Don't they have something like the Eiffel Tower though, some big Statue of Liberty type deal?"

"No, I think this is it."

"What a gyp."

They'd had lunch at the hotel and it had left them rather unimpressed. On the way back they stopped for dinner at a little restaurant along the way, and once again had a similar experience - the food was awfully bland.

"This is like the stuff my mother makes at home, it doesn't taste like anything," Larry complained.

"Nah, it could be worse," Ralph said with his mouth full.

"Frank likes it," Larry observed, watching Frank wolf it down.

"Frank likes everything," Ralph said.

After dinner, they stopped at a pub to grab some drinks and investigate the local nightlife. The girls were beautiful but rather stone-faced, they didn't seem to react to anything. Ralph had a few beers and tried to engage one of them in conversation. He started joking around about the soccer on TV, and then tried out one of his more amusing baseball anecdotes to see if it produced any results.

The girl was tall and statuesque, a middle-aged blonde. She sat there staring at him blankly, just long enough for Ralph to wonder if maybe he'd offended her somehow. Then she spoke.

"Can you amplify?" the girl said, modulating her icy disposition only slightly.

"Sorry?" he asked. She simply repeated it, then waited. Of all the girls in Copenhagen, he'd found the one who didn't speak English.

"You should tell her what happens when you amplify," Larry said, leaning closer to speak in Ralph's ear. "The audience runs screaming from the room."

"Very funny. Shut the fuck up," Ralph said.

"Goddamn chicks are made of stone though, aren't they?" Larry said, leaning back and surveying the scene. "Jesus Christ, it's like trying to talk to the wall."

"I heard it's even worse in Norway," Ralph responded, taking a drink.

"You're like the travel brochure all of a sudden. What the hell do you know about Norway?"

"Guy at the bar told me about it once."

"My ass."

The next day was the day of the festival. They had to go down in the afternoon to do a soundcheck first, so a van came by to collect their equipment and take it over in advance. Larry was falling all over himself trying to get the drums out of their boxes, banging into walls and wrestling them down the stairs. Ralph watched him dourly.

"Having a little trouble there?" he asked.

"Well you could help me with it you know, you jackass," Larry returned.

"They're your drums, you figure it out," Ralph said. Larry shot him daggers.

They got everything in the van, then went out on the street to waste some time. There were still a few hours before the soundcheck.

"I need a drink, let's hit that pub we saw yesterday," Ralph said. "It'll loosen us up a bit."

They went in and sat down. Larry ordered some European beer they had on draught.

"What the hell's this fruity shit, it's like a chick drink," he complained, making a face.

"It's Belgian, it's a wheat beer," Ralph said.

"The Belgians are a buncha fruits," Larry decided.

They drank for a little while but the tension wasn't lessening - they were all in a bad mood. Larry and Ralph sat there bickering the whole time, and even Frank looked out of sorts.

"We're gonna be shit-faced for the show if we keep this up," Larry said.

"This is the last one," Ralph said, staring down into the bottom of his glass as he drained it.

Around four, they took a taxi to the venue. The show was being held in a big park near the center of town. A sizeable stage had been set up at one end, and they headed over to it.

"Ah, hello, you must be the American band," a little guy said, rushing over to shake their hands. He was dressed in some sort of hipster getup and was a few years past his prime; he looked like a balding ferret with a ponytail.

"Yeah, we're the Americans," Ralph agreed.

"Your equipment is just over there, why don't you set up and then we'll do the sound?"

Larry worked to assemble his drum set while Ralph stood close to the front of the stage, fighting to settle his nerves. He'd been hoping the beer would do the trick, but it hadn't - now he just felt buzzed and nervous at the same time. The local techs were wandering around running cables and positioning microphones here and there.

"Ok, let's do main vocal first," said the guy sitting behind the mixer.

"Check, one two. One, two." Ralph had seen other singers do this before, he felt very professional.

They set a few more levels, then the guy asked them to play a song together to do some balancing for the group. They launched into one of the easier numbers, a blues thing they'd been playing for years. And lo and behold, Larry was slowing the beat down yet again, just as he always did. Ralph turned around to scowl at him as they went, and Larry scowled back. Ralph turned around and walked over to him when they had finished.

"You do that during the show and I'm gonna kill you," he grumbled at him under his breath.

"Shut the fuck up," Larry shot back.

"Another vocal check, main mic please," said the sound guy.

Ralph stepped up to accommodate him. Larry began to throw drum sticks at Ralph's back, one by one, fully intent on pissing him off. Ralph spun around again.

"Cut the shit Larry, I'm serious," he snarled. Larry sat there on the drum stool with a stupid grin on his face, daring him to do something.

"More main mic, please," the sound guy said.

Ralph went back to the mic. Larry threw a few more sticks.

"Check, one two. One, two."

A stick hit him square in the back of the head. Ralph snapped. He whirled around and threw his guitar at the drum kit, sending it smashing into the toms and cymbals and destroying half the set. Larry got up off the floor, picked up the snare drum and flung it at Ralph's head. Ralph fell forward, grabbing the hi-hat by the stand and swinging it like a baseball bat. The little ponytail fellow came running over.

"Hey guys, calm down, what's going on?" he said, bewildered and wondering what to do. A couple of security guards appeared.

"Okay, that's enough," one of them said, trying to grab Ralph and pull him away.

"Get off, I'm gonna kill him," Ralph said, wading through the debris and trying to get his hands on Larry as he squirmed around.

"I said that's enough," the guard said, as his partner joined the fray. Ralph swung his arm around and caught the first guard clean in the face. The ponytail guy started to yell.

***

"So how do European jails compare with American ones?" Larry asked.

"They're cleaner," Ralph said.

They were in a cell by themselves, no one else was in sight. Ralph looked around. It really was true, Danish jails were in fact much cleaner.

In an hour or so, a guard came to get them. "Your friend is here," he said tersely. They followed the guard to the front, signed some paperwork and then went out through the double doors. Frank was there with a taxi, waiting for them.

"Where the hell did Frank get money for a cab? I thought he was broke," Larry wondered as they approached.

"No idea, maybe his mother gave it to him for the trip," Ralph said. Larry thought about it for a few seconds.

"Or maybe he steals the money off the collection plate at church and doesn't tell anyone about it."

"Unlikely, but possible."

They went back to the hotel. They'd been told the charges were to be dropped, pending their immediate departure from the country. Their hosts had been so kind as to return their equipment to the room already, it was all sitting there in a nice tidy pile in the corner. Needless to say, they'd missed the festival and would not be playing in it.

The following morning they went to the airport, got on the plane and in short order were back home in Jersey again. Ralph and Larry weren't speaking to each other. Ralph holed up in his apartment and did nothing for three straight days. Then Gina called.

"So how'd it go?" she asked.

"I tried to kill Larry and they sent us home," Ralph said. Raucous laughter ensued, he had to take the receiver away from his ear.

"What kind of a fucking moron does that?" she said.

"Gina, I'm tired. What do you want?"

"I broke up with my boyfriend," Gina said, now popping her gum into the phone.

"Sorry to hear that," Ralph said.

"No you're not," she said.

"Actually you're right. Does this mean you're going to bug me more often?"

"Yes. When you guys going over to Willy's again?"

"Never. It burned down."

"Why do you have to be such a - "

Ralph hung up the phone.

On Monday morning, he drove down to the temp agency. They didn't have anything for him, but they said they'd call if something came up. Back to this shit again. Ralph drove over to the place on the corner and got himself a coffee, then took it outside on the sidewalk with him. The sun was out and it was unseasonably warm. Where to go next.

He took a long leisurely stroll over to the park and sat down on a bench. An old man was sitting nearby.

"Enjoying the weather?" the old-timer asked.

"I am," Ralph said. "Pretty warm for end of October, isn't it?"

"It is indeed. It's supposed to get colder next week though, I hear. You live around here, young fellar?" the old man asked, eager to make conversation and sliding over on his bench to hear better.

"Yeah, I've got an apartment over there," he said, nodding in no particular direction.

"What do you do for a living?" the man asked.

"I'm a musician," Ralph replied after a brief pause.

"No kidding. What instrument do you play?"

"I play guitar. My band just had a show over in Denmark, actually."

"Wow, Denmark, that's impressive. And how'd it go?"

"Well... we had some problems."

"Sorry to hear that. Life throws you a lot of curveballs, doesn't it?"

"It sure does."

"It's how you deal with 'em that counts."

"The breaking balls are even worse," Ralph said with a crooked grin, wondering if he'd get the joke. The old man smiled back at him.

The conversation lapsed, and then almost by silent mutual agreement they both sat back to soak in the sun and enjoy the surroundings. The birds were chirping, the squirrels were scampering around in the trees, a few little kids were running back and forth with mothers nearby. It was nice just sitting there. Maybe this was enough, maybe all the rest of it was just bullshit, Ralph thought. Maybe he'd go find himself a place on a beach somewhere and become a bum, or maybe he'd go live in a cave. But the park bench was just fine for now.

Time drifted by. After a while Ralph stirred, and then got up. "Well it was nice talkin' to ya," he said to the guy with a smile and a little wave.

"Enjoy the rest of your day," the old man said. "And good luck with your music." He looked happy just to have had someone to talk to. Ralph wandered back to the car, went home and got the mail. Baseball season was over, no more Mets games for a while. He fixed himself a snack and sat down on the couch to relax.

***

The next day was Saturday. Ralph got up bright and early and went to get breakfast at McDonalds. He didn't feel like doing the drive-thru, so he went inside for a change, picking up a newspaper from the metal bin along the way. He sat down and read as he ate. There was a lot going on, the world was falling apart.

Then he went back to the apartment, turned on some music and sat on the floor to listen to it. It sounded good, so he turned it up a little more - fuck the mechanic if he didn't like it. Everything was off-limits, all the time, he was tired of it.

Larry came by around noon - there was a thump on the pole outside and then the buzzer rang. Ralph thought about not answering it, then decided what the hell. Larry clumped heavily up the stairs and came in through the door. "Look, I'm sorry about what happened, all right," he said immediately.

"Me too. Don't worry about it," Ralph said. He went into the kitchen, got a couple of beers and handed one to Larry.

"This couch is falling apart, when you gonna get a new one," Larry said as he sat down on it.

"Nothing wrong with it, it's just got a few holes."

"You seen Frank?"

"Nah, he hasn't been around. You?"

"No, me neither. I think his mother's sick."

"How do you know that?"

"I heard her coughing last time I went over there. He disappears every time she gets sick, you know, he sticks around to take care of her until she gets better."

"He's a good kid, that Frank," said Ralph. "We should go get him anyway and go for a drink tonight, what do you think?"

"Sounds like a plan."

They went to Willy's that night. It was an off night for some reason, not too many people around. Henry had the door open and a cool breeze was blowing in. Henry was bored and came over to talk.

"Hey, so tell me more about the big trip to Europe. How did it go, you enjoy yourselves?" he asked them as he leaned against the bar.

"Didn't go so good," Larry said. "Ralph blew it."

Ralph turned to scowl at him, so in the interest of staving off disaster he added, "Just kidding."

"What did you think of Denmark?" Henry asked.

"It's cold, but the chicks are hot," Larry said.

"It's expensive," Ralph said.

"The food sucks," Larry added. "Oh, and they have a little mermaid in the water, it's about the size of your fist."

"Well, what are you gonna do," Henry mused, waxing philosophical as he shuffled off to wash a few more glasses. "Different strokes for different folks and all that, you know what they say."

"Did Gina call?" Larry asked Ralph.

"Of course she did."

"What did she say?"

"What does she ever say, she babbles. She told me she broke up with her boyfriend."

"You should go tell Frank."

"Shut the fuck up." Ralph took a swig of beer.

Larry had confirmed earlier that Frank's Mom was in fact sick. Ralph leaned back to talk to him around Larry.

"Hey Frank, how's your Mom doing?" Frank waggled his hand back and forth, giving him the so-so sign. He looked tired.

"Frank's Mom is sick," he told Henry.

"Everybody's sick, everyone who comes in here right now. Always happens when the weather changes."

There were no chicks in there that night. Ralph and Larry went over to shoot a few games of pool, then put some money in the jukebox.

"Play something good," Larry said.

Ralph put five bucks in, bluesy stuff from the seventies, good drinking music. Then they went back and got another round of beers.

"Henry, your dartboards are falling apart," Larry said as Henry passed by.

"No shit. I've been telling Mike about that for months now, you try telling him."

Ralph sat at the bar pensively for a while, then stirred.

"We should start practicing again soon," he said.

"You gotta be shittin' me," Larry said in disbelief, almost letting go of the bottle. "Are you insane?"

"Look, it was an off night," Ralph said. "We can do better than that."

"It wasn't a night at all, we never even made it to the fuckin' gig," Larry said.

"Yeah I know that, but shit happens. I know this guy I've been talking to who says there's an opening for weeknights at a place called The Outhouse, over in Denville."

"That's out in the fucking sticks," Larry laughed.

"What the hell does that matter?" Ralph cried indignantly. "It's a gig, we're trying to play music here right? But anyway, the point I'm making is that we gotta keep it going, we shouldn't just quit."

"Yes we should," Larry said.

Ralph went back to his beer. It didn't matter what Larry said, he wasn't giving up. Everyone had their bad days now and then, they'd just stay away from Denmark this time. Someday they'd get lucky, they'd catch a break. And it was going to happen soon, Ralph could feel it in his bones. Even the sun shines on a dog's ass some days.

A year passed, and then another one. The band got back together again but only half-heartedly, continuing on their steady path to nowhere. Ralph had been blackballed from the IT world entirely, word having gotten out that he was insane. Computer work now out of the question, he picked up odd jobs here and there, little shitty things, whatever came up with the temp agency mostly. Organizing shelves and pushing heavy objects around. He'd bought himself an old secondhand push mower which he stored in Larry's parent's garage and used it to cut lawns from time to time. Apart from that, there was nothing going on. At all. Life had slowed to an absolute crawl. Sometimes it almost seemed to stop.

It was the middle of July, and hot. Ralph had just mowed another lawn, his second one of the day. He'd dropped the thing off at Larry's parent's house, gone back to the apartment and cracked open a beer, what would inevitably be the first of many. Larry followed soon after. He was driving slightly better these days, managing to avoid the pole more often than not.

"So how's the lawn-mowing business?" Larry asked, getting his own beer and sitting down.

"Sucks," Ralph said. "'I've never hated lawns so much in my entire life. The sight of grass makes me sick."

"Better than being homeless," Larry observed, taking a slug.

"Debatable," Ralph said.

"We goin' to Willy's on Friday?"

"I guess. I'm getting tired of that place, to be honest."

Larry sat up, offended. "What? Get the fuck outta here. How could anyone get tired of Willy's? The place is an institution. Besides, what else are we gonna do on a Friday night?"

"Not go there."

"And? Then what?"

"Don't start."

Larry let it drop. They'd gotten into a wrestling match in the middle of Seventh Avenue the other day and he wasn't in the mood for any more.

"What's Gina up to these days?" he asked.

"She had some new guy, lasted all of about a week. She was all hot and bothered, wouldn't shut up about it and now he's already gone again. Dumb fuck probably sobered up and got a good look at her."

At Willy's on Friday, Frank was in a funk.

"Frank's is a funk," Ralph said to Larry.

They watched him as he did his hangdog routine, his head drooping forward like he was trying to drown in his beer mug.

"What's his problem?" Larry asked. "He looked fine yesterday."

"Maybe his Mom's sick again."

"Nah, she's fine. Saw her yesterday too."

"He needs some more excitement in his life."

"He needs to get laid."

Larry refrained from adding anything about Gina's newfound availability, as the joke had gotten somewhat stale.

Ralph sat there and pondered. *He* needed some excitement in his life too, for Chrissake. He was tired of everything going nowhere, of nothing ever happening, of sitting around on his ass, waiting for the end of the world like every other poor dumb schmuck. Something needed to change, that much was clear. He went home and let it rattle around in his head a little more, wondering what could be done. Then it came to him, hitting him like a ton of bricks as he lay there in bed. The next morning he broke the news to Larry over coffee.

"I've got it. We're going to rob a bank," he said, sitting down at the table across from him.

"Stop being an idiot," Larry said, refusing to dignify the comment with so much as an upward glance.

"No, I'm serious. The money is just sitting there on the other side of some fuckin' wall somewhere, just waiting for someone to come along and pick it up. The way I see it, it might as well be us."

"You're not serious, you're an idiot. Look Ralph, no offense, but you have trouble making toast. How the fuck are you going to rob a bank?"

"Oh yeah, look who's talking," Ralph grumbled. "Says the guy who can't walk into a room without falling over. But no, listen, it's probably pretty easy. All we need is a drill."

Larry laughed at that one. "A *drill*? How's that supposed to work? You mean, going in through the wall? Why not use your pocket knife. Listen to this guy," Larry trailed off, still chuckling into his coffee.

"I've seen it work before."

"On TV."

"If it works on TV, that means they had to get the idea from somewhere, right? Besides, I think I read about it in the papers one time too, a crew of guys who pulled it off in Brooklyn or somewhere."

"You know, you're really crazy, you know that? And then we get busted and go to jail again, but prison this time, the big house, not like your little Denmark type deal there. You know how long you'd last in fuckin' prison? About five minutes, that's how long."

"We won't get caught though. Not if we do it right."

Larry shook his head. "Listen to this guy," he said again. "Thinks he's Bonnie and Clyde over here. Maybe we could get Gina to drive the getaway car."

But Ralph worked on him over time and soon had him at least entertaining the possibility that it could work. They were leaving Frank out of it for now, unsure of what his reaction would be. Frank was mellow, go-with-the-flow and all that, but he was occasionally unpredictable and this was breaking some seriously new ground. Ralph was saying there was a place in Hackensack that had lax security, that didn't even have the cameras and alarms set up right. A guy who'd worked there had told him about it at the bar one night, he said. And there was a dark alley in back where they could set up alongside the wall and not be bothered while they worked. The two of them chewed over the idea for a week or two, letting it settle in, allowing it to percolate for awhile.

"You gotta admit, it would be nice having some money for a change," Ralph would say over beers, trying to get further into Larry's head. Larry wouldn't respond, but he wouldn't argue either, at least not right away. But then common sense would prevail and he'd just laugh it off like before.

They went into the city one weekend with Gina and they'd all gotten drunk. Then Larry had let the plan slip as they sat there at the bar, in spite of his better judgment.

"You know what this crazy guy wants to do? He wants to rob a bank. It's all he's talked about for the last month," Larry said, leaning heavily into Gina as he confided in her.

"Shut the fuck up Larry," Ralph warned immediately, teeth clenched and growling like a bear, but it was too late.

"Hahahahahaha!!" Gina said, spitting her beer out. "That's fuckin' hilarious! Shithead couldn't tie his own shoes without directions! How you gonna rob a bank?!"

"That's what I told him," Larry said.

"Larry, what the hell is wrong with you," Ralph said in a low voice, talking right into his ear. "I told you not to tell anyone about it. You're gonna screw everything up."

"Okay, double-oh-seven, go back to your beer," Larry said, waving him off.

But Ralph was pissed. The last person on earth they needed to know about this was Gina, it would be all over the news before it even happened. Ralph looked over at Frank to see what sort of impression it had made there, but Frank didn't look affected one way or the other. He was pretty damn drunk, might not have even heard what they'd said. Then again, he'd always been a hard book to read.

Back at the apartment, he thought about it some more. And some more. He thought about it over lunch, he thought about it over the Mets game, thought about it over dinner and the whole time he was trying to sleep. It was the only thing he could think about. I mean, in theory it was so easy - you just went over there and put a hole in the wall when no one else was looking and the treasure was yours for the taking. And if what this guy was saying was true, with the cameras and alarms all wonky like they were supposed to be, then there really wouldn't be too much of a problem. The main problem was getting Larry on board, he couldn't do it alone. It was at least a two man job, probably three. Frank was dead weight, he'd go along wherever you dragged him, he was no problem. And they had to keep the shit away from Gina, that was the other thing. Her and her mouth, that would be the end of it right there, they'd have it up on billboards before the thing even gotten started. Drunk or not, Larry made one more offhand comment at the bar like that and Ralph was going to bust his ass.

They were in the city the following weekend, shooting pool at the Mexican place over on the West Side.

"Why do we come here," Larry groused. "This place is a shithole."

"Because the beer's cheap," Ralph said. He pocketed a few more balls and then started in again. "Okay, so I found this drill we can use."

Larry let the stick roll out of his hand and onto the floor. "You need to stop with this shit, you really do. It's not healthy."

"No, seriously."

Larry sighed. "And where did you find this drill?"

"In the Sears catalog."

Disbelief. "The Sears catalog?"

"Yeah." A pause. "What's wrong with that?"

"What are you, fixing the sink? The Sears catalog. You've gotta be kidding me."

"Look, it's one of those big industrial models, the ones they use on construction jobs. It pokes holes in the wall the size of your head. All we need to do is put a few holes through and then we can punch out the rest, with a sledgehammer or something."

"You know how much noise that's gonna make, you maniac? It's Hackensack, it's not like we're out in the middle of nowhere."

"So that's why we do it late at night, and why we go back in the alley where there's no one else around."

"Dude, someone's still gonna hear it."

One of the locals bumped into Larry from behind, mumbling objections as he did so.

"What did he say?" Larry asked, looking over his shoulder.

"It was in Mexican, don't worry about it. So, what do you think?"

"The same thing I thought yesterday, and the day before, and the day before that. That you're completely insane. Who the fuck wants to rob a bank anyway?"

"Fortune favors the bold," said Ralph, albeit with a deeply perturbed frown as he bent over for another shot.

"Fortune my ass. A lengthy jail sentence favors the bold. It would be one thing if we knew what in the hell we were doing, but we don't. I deliver pizzas, you mow lawns. Frank doesn't do anything at all. And you're going to break in through the wall of some bank and run off with all the money, just like that? If it were that fuckin' easy, don't you think everyone and his mom would be doing it?"

"Most people lack imagination."

"No, most people are in touch with reality. I'm telling you, you need to lay off with this crap. It's gonna get you in trouble."

"Stop being such a pussy. You know as well as I do there's a pretty good chance this can work, I can tell by listening to you. Okay, so how bout this - we go over there some time early next week and just case the joint out a little bit, get the lay of the land and see how it looks. Then we'll have a better idea of what we're dealing with."

Larry snickered. "'Case the joint out', I swear you've been watching too many gangster movies. But okay, fine, just for shits and giggles we'll go over there and 'case the joint out'. Maybe it'll knock some sense into you."

* * *

And then just when he thought he had everything in his head pointing in the right general direction, his mother called.

"Oh, no," Ralph said, holding the phone at arm's length before returning it to his ear. It had been a while since their last sparring session.

"Did you call your Uncle Richard?"

"No Ma, I haven't yet."

"Why not? I thought you said you were going to call him. He's your only uncle, you know, it wouldn't hurt for you to call him on his birthday."

"Yes Ma, I know."

"Then why didn't you call?"

"Because I forgot."

"You *forgot*? What do you mean, you *forgot*? You know, you can be so selfish sometimes, Ralph. He was always so nice to you, he brought you candy and all sorts of things when you were growing up. The least you could do is call him once a year for his birthday. I mean, it's not that big a deal, is it? You could think about other people every now and then too."

"I know, Ma."

"So are you going to call?"

"Yes, Ma."

"When?"

"I'll call him today."

She paused to reload.

"Okay... Well, the reason I called was that your sister wants you to watch Davey for a few hours this weekend while she goes to do some shopping. Normally we would do it, but your father isn't feeling well and we don't want to get him sick. So can you do it, can you watch Davey for a little while on Saturday?"

"Mmmmmm, I dunno Ma."

"You don't know? What's that supposed to mean? Why not?"

"Well, I mean, I've got some things going on right now."

There was haughty Queen-Of-France laughter going on in the background now. This was where it really got going. Ralph bit the receiver in anticipation. She was talking to his father now, yelling at him across the room.

"He says he 'has something going on.' Do you believe this?" There was a bestial grunt in response and then she returned to her original target.

"You know Ralph, we do all sorts of things for you and all we ask in return is for you to help out a little bit every now and then. I mean, is that too much to ask? It's just for a little while! A few hours, that's all we're asking. You can't step away for a few hours from all this important stuff you have going on and watch Davey? I just don't understand you sometimes. Rachel is your only sister and you practically never see her, and now when she has one little thing to ask of you, one little favor and of course you have to..."

Ralph's head was on fire. He could speak no more. Time passed. The words on the other end eventually fizzled out.

"Hello?" his mother quacked.

"I'm here, Ma."

"*Well???* Are you going to do it or not?"

"Okay, I'll think about it."

"'You'll think about it.' Oh, well la-di-da. We wouldn't want to inconvenience His Highness, now would we? What do you have going on right now that's so important anyway?"

"Larry and I are working on something."

"Something for work?"

".....Yeah, something like that."

"You don't want to tell me what it is?"

"No."

"Why not?"

The static hissing in Ralph's ears was like a kettle about to boil. Like a massive locomotive pulling out from the station. Like the wind from some fearsome storm, rushing through the tall grass of the prairie, just before the tornado got started. It was worse than that, it was the loudest fucking hissing noise in the history of hissing noises. It was a great serpent, a thousand miles long, a cosmic beast of vengeance come to devour the world, just to put an end to the sounds his mother was making.

"Because... it's a secret, okay, Ma? I don't have to tell you everything."

"Aaaaand here we go with the attitude. You know Ralph, I put up with a lot from you, and I don't normally say anything about it but - "

The phone went sailing across the room. It crashed into the wall next to the window and fell down, silent at last. Another few inches and it would have smashed the glass and continued right on out into the street. His whole life was one big bitching session. There were times when Ralph thought about not answering the phone anymore at all - I mean what was the point, it was never good news. But that would just mean she'd start coming over to the apartment in person, and we couldn't have that happening either. There were bad options and worse options. You picked your poison and then spit back in its eye.

His sister came over on Saturday with Davey. He'd agreed to do it after all. The kid could be a little shit when he was in the wrong mood, but he was okay for the most part. Rachel dropped him off with a few parting words and then left. Ralph and the kid stood there staring at each other, squaring off.

"I wanna watch TV," Davey said.

"Knock yourself out," Ralph said, grabbing the clicker and turning it on, relieved it wasn't something else. "What do you want to watch?"

"Sponge Bob."

"I don't think I have that," Ralph said, already confused, clicking around through the channels.

"You don't have Sponge Bob? Don't you have normal TV?"

"Nope."

"Why not?"

"Jesus Christ, you sound like your grandmother." Ralph kept clicking until he found another cartoon and the kid settled down.

"Your apartment is small," Davey said, looking around the room.

"Yes, it is," Ralph replied.

"And it's dirty too," Davey observed.

"Listen kid, I'll tell you in advance that I don't like children very much. I once got fired from a job because I almost strangled one of them. It happened twice, in fact."

Davey was unfazed. "You're weird, Uncle Ralph."

"Do you want a drink?" Ralph asked him.

"Yes, please."

"What do you want?"

"What do you have?"

"I have beer."

"That's it?"

"And water."

"From the tap?"

"Yes."

"That's it?"

"That's it."

"Can't I have juice?"

"There is no juice, I just told you."

"Mommy always has juice at home."

"Good for Mommy."

"I want juice."

Ralph got up grumbling, took a big chunk of sugar from the cabinet, dumped it in some water and put the glass in Davey's hand.

"That's not juice! That's water with some sugar in it."

"Pretend."

Davey sipped at his sugar water. "How come you don't have a girlfriend?" he asked.

"Because the last one damn near did me in."

"What does that mean?"

"Never mind."

"Mommy says you're never going to get married."

"She is correct."

Davey continued inspecting the room, his eyes roaming far and wide. "You don't have a lot of furniture," he concluded.

"I know that," Ralph said.

"How come?"

"Davey, I'm going to put you in the closet. Please, just pipe down for awhile."

Davey got up and started wandering around the room. Ralph heard strings vibrating on a guitar, the old acoustic on its stand in the corner.

"Don't touch that," Ralph fired over.

"I just want to play it," Davey said.

"You can't."

"Can you play it?"

"Yes. Well, sort of. Depends on who you ask."

"Were you ever in a band?"

"I'm in one now."

"With who else?"

"A couple of morons. Davey, quit with the questions, please. Uncle Ralph needs to rest."

Davey stayed for the rest of the afternoon. They went over to the park, threw the football around for an hour or so and then Rachel came and picked him up again. Fine, that was over with - now he could get back to business. What they needed were schematics. If they had a better idea of the layout of the bank, like where the vault was at and shit like that, there was a much better chance of success.

"I wonder how you get schematics for a bank," Ralph mused as he sat with Larry at the bar the next night.

"Schematics? You mean, like blueprints?"

"Yeah. To get the layout of the place."

Larry started to respond, then restrained himself. To respond would be to humor him. No need to pour any more gas on the fire.

"Ralph, I think you should see someone," he said finally, finishing his beer and signaling to Henry for another one.

Ralph was ignoring him, lost in space, but eventually came back to what had been said. "What?"

"I said, I think you should see someone. A shrink or something. This is becoming one hell of an obsession with you."

"Whadd're you talking about?"

"Just what I said. You're cracking up." Larry turned to Frank. "Frank, he's cracking up, right?" Frank smiled cryptically, it looked like a yes. Larry had filled him in on the plan a few days earlier, over Ralph's strenuous objections.

"C'mon Frank, you know this could work just as well as I do," Ralph objected, formally looping him into the conspiracy. "You heard about the alarms and all that shit, right? Seriously, what do you think about it?" Frank shrugged, now it looked like a maybe.

Ralph got mad. "What the fuck does Frank know anyway. What is he supposed to be, some authority on the subject or something ? And I'm gettin' sick and tired of your crap too, Larry. If you want to be in on this, then you better start getting with the program."

Larry choked on his beer, dribbling half of it down his shirt. "The program, do you hear this?" But he was through arguing, at least for now. He downed the rest of the new beer in one gulp, then got up to use the bathroom. "You explain it to him, Frank," he said, patting him on the shoulder on the way there.

Another few days and then it was Gina's turn. She came over the apartment and plopped herself down on the couch.

"I need to ask you a favor," she said.

Jesus Christ, what was with all the favors lately. Ralph frowned hard. "What is it, Gina."

"I need you to be my date on Friday night."

"What? No."

"Come on, Ralph," she whined. "It'll be fun."

"No, it absolutely will not."

"Come on, Ralph. Stop screwing around."

This required a beer. He went to the fridge to get one. There was a certain look in

Gina's eye, something verging on vulnerable, and on the spur of the moment he actually grabbed a second bottle and brought it out to her.

"So why do you need a date on Friday night?"

"There's this guy down at the Pinnacle who I'm trying to impress."

"Aha. So this is the one, eh? You've found the one you want?"

"Yeah. I want to get in his pants real bad." She was trying to joke around and it wasn't funny, she already had Ralph squirming on the couch. "I want to make like ten little babies with him and let him whisk me off to the Philippines or someplace."

"Your grand dream finally realized."

"So will you go with me?"

"I told you, no."

"Whaddya mean, no?" Gina sat up. "Ralph, I need your help here." She tried whining, she tried pleading, she got nowhere. Then a devilish look flickered across her face. "I'm going to fuck Frank if you don't take me to the Pinnacle on Friday night."

That one got Ralph's attention. She sounded serious. "That's not funny, Gina."

"I'm gonna do it. I'm gonna fuck Frank if you don't take me over there. I'm gonna fuck him right in the ass."

"You and that mouth."

Gina was giggling now, but Ralph couldn't tell if she was actually serious about it or not. The old imagery popped into his head again, of having to sit there at the bar with them as some newly-formed couple or something. It was intolerable.

"Okay, fine, I'll do it."

Gina jumped up with a gleeful squeal, waving her arms around like a little kid. "See you Friday," she said, disappearing through the doorway.

Friday night came and Gina showed up around seven. She was dressed in a skirt and high heels and had her hair done up all fancy.

"High heels? Isn't that a bit much?"

"Why? I told you, I'm gonna seal the deal tonight."

"What's this guy's name?'

"Chris."

"Have you ever even talked to him before?"

"Not really. But he's looked at me a few times."

They got in the car and drove into the city. Gina lit a cigarette, she was nervous. She was so nervous she was quiet for a while. She was on her third cigarette by the time they reached the parking garage in Manhattan.

"What's the point of getting all dolled up like that if you're going to smell like an ashtray?" Ralph asked her.

But Gina didn't respond. She wasn't to be distracted that night - she was in the zone, she had her game face on and was ready for battle. Ralph escorted her down the street as she tottered along on her spiky heels and they found the place. Ralph had only been in there once before and it had been full of twits, but tonight it was a little looser, a little more relaxed. And sure enough, there was the clique of military guys at the far end of the bar, looking big and burly. A few of them were even wearing their uniforms.

"Which one is yours?" Ralph asked as they ordered drinks from the bartender.

"That one there," Gina said, pointing him out, whispering for no good reason.

"What a hunk," Ralph said sarcastically.

Again she didn't respond. Most unusual. Ralph had never seen Gina take anything seriously before, it was almost spooky to watch. Her eyes were trained on her prey like a tigress eyeing a gazelle, unblinking and absolutely laser-focused. Ralph kept expecting that dry raspy tongue to come out and lick her lips but it didn't happen. She turned back to the bar and downed her sex on the beach. "I need another drink," she said, pointedly half-turning his way.

"Gina, I'm not buying your drinks tonight. Let that guy do it."

"Cheap ass fucker."

"Where are all those goofy friends of yours? I thought they were always here with you."

"I told them to stay away tonight."

Ralph took another look at this guy Chris. He was a wannabe military wife's wet dream. His hair was perfect, his uniform neatly pressed, his little buttons and medals and things all polished to a nice bright shine; he radiated self-confidence, along with a firm, manly vitality, a potent life force that bespoke an ability to procreate. His glances round the room were friendly yet condescending, as if he owned the joint along with everything in it. This guy had never made a mistake in his life. He was like Mr. Wilkinson with a little more testosterone thrown in. One look at him and Ralph knew Gina had no shot. There was a chance it might even get ugly. But what was he supposed to do about it, Gina was going to do what she was going to do. She was a big girl, she had a mind of her own. He sat back and prepared to watch the show.

Gina had two more drinks and then was ready to make her move. Chris hadn't looked over in their direction even once and Ralph could tell it was driving Gina crazy: if he was supposed to be jealous by now, there certainly weren't any signs of it. But Gina was on a mission from God, not to be deterred under any circumstances. Ralph watched as she rounded the corner of the bar, then pulled up short, hesitating for just a moment as she reached her destination, waffling before this steaming pile of muscle-flexing smugness. Chris pretended she wasn't there for a moment, then, realizing something had to be said, begrudgingly turned towards Gina with a patronizing smirk and readied to direct some of his precious attention her way.

Ralph couldn't hear what was being said, but he could tell from a distance that Gina was going all out - she was really turning on the charm, batting those long fake eyelashes at him and oohing and aahing all over the place, laughing at every stupid thing he said. If this guy had only known what Gina was really like, the way she was normally when she wasn't hitting on someone, he would have been laughing his head off. They went back and forth with the chitchat but it clearly wasn't working. Gina fought the good fight for a few minutes, trying to hold on as long as possible. She babbled on and on until the douchebag got tired of it, and then one of Gina's hated blondes moved in and that was that.

Gina drifted back over, crushed. Ralph bought her another drink.

"Here, drink this," he said, putting it in front of her.

But she was inconsolable, beyond the powers of speech. She put one drink down, and then another, and then another, and by the time it was last call Ralph was practically carrying her down the street. He'd kept himself pretty sober in case Gina got crazy, in case she made some kind of big scene. She kept it together until they got in the car and were on their way home and then she let loose, the floodgates opened.

"*I don't understand*!" she bawled.

"Come on, honey, it happens to the best of us. You win some, you lose some. Maybe you just weren't his type."

Shit, wrong comment. Ralph knew it before it even got free of his mouth, but there was no recalling it. Gina bawled even louder now, howling like a castrated monkey. "Shut up, you asshole!!!" she shrieked.

"No, look - what I'm trying to say is - I mean, what do you even see in that guy? He's a gigantic douchebag, I don't even need to say two words to him to be able to tell. He's got a huge sign on him that says 'Gigantic Douchebag'."

Gina laughed a little at this. Ralph breathed a slight sigh of relief, she was starting to relax. She took a tissue out of her bag and dabbed at her eyes with it, wiping some of the streaking mascara away, sweeping the tears to both sides. "Thanks for coming with me tonight, Ralph." She smiled at him with big doe eyes, looking like a scarecrow from hell.

They got back to the apartment and before Ralph could even shut the door Gina was throwing her arms around his neck, still sloppy drunk.

"Let's go in the other room," she slurred in his ear.

"I don't think that's a good idea," Ralph said, trying to fend her off.

But she was insistent, and in her present fragile state Ralph figured he'd have to take one for the team here. He took her into the bedroom, laid her on the bed and they did the deed.

In the morning, Gina rolled over.

"Was it good?" she asked.

"As good as it always was," Ralph said.

Gina thought about saying more but couldn't decide if it had been meant as a compliment or an insult. Ralph yawned and stretched. "You know, I think that's the first time we've ever had sex when I was sober."

Gina tried getting up but couldn't, falling back over in a groaning heap. "Go make some coffee," she said.

***

"So I hear you and Gina are back together again," Larry said.

"God damn it, does that girl ever stop talking," Ralph said.   "We're not back together. It was a booty call. When the hell did you talk to her anyway?"

"Hey Henry, Ralph and Gina are back together again," Larry called down the bar.

"Good to hear," Henry called back.

Ralph ignored it. "Where's Frank?" he asked.

"On his way over," Larry said.

Things still weren't sitting well. "No really, how do you know? Frank didn't tell you, did he?"

"How? Through morse code?"

Ralph was still glowering. "She was in here the other day," Larry said.

"Lovely. And she told the whole bar."

"No, just me."

More glowering. Larry smiled. "Don't worry, I'm not going to hit on your girlfriend."

"She's not my girlfriend. And do not refer to her as such when she's around, or you'll give her ideas."

They postponed taking a look at the bank for a bit, as Larry suddenly had prior engagements.   He wouldn't elaborate on what those were, he just said 'prior engagements'.   Ralph stewed in his juices impatiently. He drank beer and watched TV and waited. He went out for coffee, he went out for food. He went to McDonalds to get a burger and fries. They still hadn't fixed the goddamn squawking intercom box. The girl buzzed at him like a fly and he growled back.

"Why can't you people fix this goddamn box," he said.

The buzzing revealed nothing further. He drove around to pick up his food.

"You know, you guys obviously aren't taking me seriously, but I'm not kidding - I can't understand a single solitary word you're saying to me over that thing. I mean, I don't know what the point of having it is. You might as well be speaking in Yiddish."

The girl stared him down sourly. It was a different girl than before, only slightly less rotund. She had a little bow in her hair. Ralph was feeling ornery, he wasn't done yet.

"Doesn't it bother you at all that you're completely wasting your breath back there, whenever you talk to people?"

"Sir, I make about five bucks an hour. Do you really think I care if the intercom works or not?"

"God damn it", Ralph muttered under his breath, snatching the bag out of her hand

and speeding off. This was what was wrong with the world. No accountability. If they kept up with this shit, one day he was going to go back there with a baseball bat and knock the box right off its stand. Vigilante justice or something. A man had a right to know how much his fucking Happy Meal cost.

He called Larry up. "Come on, Larry, it's time. Get your ass in gear, let's go over there and take a look."

"Next week, next week," Larry said. "I've still got too much shit to do. Oh, and by the way, I forgot to mention - Gina wants to go to the beach this weekend. And she's bringing her friends with her."

Ralph did a double take over the phone. "Since when are you Gina's appointed spokesperson? Why am I suddenly hearing all this Gina shit through you?"

"Dunno. She's been coming down to the bar more often, that's probably it right there."

Ralph called Gina up. "Since when do I hear everything about you through Larry?"

"Since I figured out how much it pisses you off," laughed Gina, popping her gum into the phone for added effect. "Did Larry tell you, about the beach?"

"Yeah. He said you want to go."

"And I'm bringing a few friends with me."

"Fine."

Ralph hung up the phone. This was some bullshit right here. They had time to go to the beach on the weekend but they couldn't go over to the bank for an hour. Larry was taking him for a ride. The way things were going, they'd never rob the fucking thing. He wanted that money in his pocket by the end of summer, at the very latest.

The weekend arrived without delay and then they were heading down the Parkway and dodging through traffic, six of them all jammed into one car, girls in back and boys in front. Ralph was the only one with a car that would make it that far and so he was the designated driver. There was a whole lot of babbling going on and it was seriously messing with Ralph's hangover, he wished they'd all just get out and walk.

They got to the beach, parked the car and wandered out into the crowd. The sun was just ridiculously hot, the hottest day of the year, and nobody seemed to be noticing but Larry - he was complaining the entire time, bitching like an old woman. There was one girl for every guy there, which was rather convenient, and everyone had already paired up nicely. Larry's girl was a bimbo, a complete airhead without a single marble rolling around in her pretty little skull, and Frank's girl was just as quiet as he was, barely saying a word. Ralph assumed that Gina was supposed to be with him. She held his arm as they sashayed along the boardwalk and he let her.

"Ohhhh, they have hot dogs!" Larry's chick enthused. "I want one!"

What kind of a fucking airhead is surprised to find hot dogs at the Jersey shore, Ralph thought to himself. He almost said it out loud.

The group went over and got hot dogs and sodas.

"How ya holding up there, Larry," Gina asked over her shoulder as they waited in line.

"I'm melting," Larry said.

His girl seemed to have taken quite a liking to him and there was a whole lot of coy smiling and batting of eyes going on.

"Isn't the beach great?" she said. "My parents used to take us here practically every weekend during the summer when we were kids."

"Tell her all about how much you love the beach, Larry," Ralph murmured sarcastically in Larry's ear, behind a shielding hand.

"Quiet, I'm working here," Larry said.

He flashed another cheshire cat grin at the girl and she flashed it right back. Love was in the air.

They finished their food and then shambled forward into the sand, finding a place to sit not far from the water. The beach was packed. People were all over the place, playing with kids, playing with dogs, scampering to and fro.

"Look at them, they're all having such a good time," Gina said. "Don't they look happy, Ralph?"

"Can't stand them," Ralph said, glaring like Scrooge.

"Ralph's a misanthrope," Larry told his girl.

"What's a mizz-ann-throwp?" the girl asked.

"It means you hate people," Larry said.

"It means your eyes are open," Ralph mumbled.

"I love people," Larry's chick said. "I think they're nice."

Gina was sitting with her body pressed up against Ralph's, laughing at the whole thing, enjoying his discomfort immensely. "Such a bitter old man," she said, playfully poking him in the ribs.

"I'm going to go bury my head in the sand," Ralph said, starting to dig a hole.

"No wait, we'll bury you!" Gina squeaked, pushing him down and starting to shovel sand on top of him.

"No, Gina, stop, I'm not in the mood..." he moaned, pushing the sand off as quickly as she could apply it. "Bury Frank instead."

Frank was laying right next to them. All three girls converged on him at once and within sixty seconds he had been embedded in the earth's crust. All you could see was a little nose sticking out and a set of wide smiling teeth.

They went in and out of the water for a few hours and then fought their way back through the traffic.

"The last time we were here, Ralph was talking about moving to Wyoming," Larry informed the group.

"Wyoming? Why, what's in Wyoming?" asked the bimbo.

"Cows," Gina said.

"So I guess you like cows or something?" the girl asked Ralph, her voice high and dreamy.

He looked at her to see if she was kidding, but she wasn't. Trying to come up with some sort of response and failing miserably, he held his breath and turned red instead. In his mind's eye he could picture her head filling with air, slowly inflating like a rubber balloon with her facial features stretching wider by the second, growing and growing until it blotted out the sky. Like with Mr. Wilkinson, but without the magma this time.

"Do you like cows, Ralph?" Gina asked him again, needling him.

"I dated *you*, didn't I?" he blurted, the air going out of him. This got a good laugh out of Larry and Frank. Larry's girl didn't get it.

When they got home, Ralph called Larry on the phone. "Well, didja get her number?" he asked.

"Yep. Going out with her some time next week."

"Nicely done," Ralph said appreciatively. "Not bad looking either."

"Yeah, but I'm going to have to talk to her at some point. I'm not sure she can count to ten.

***

Another week went by. "All right Larry, that's enough," Ralph said. "We're going to the bank tomorrow."

"Fine, let's get it over with," Larry said into the phone. "Should we bring Frank with us?"

"I don't care."

"Might as well. After all, he might be in on the big heist with us."

Larry was still having trouble believing he was even playing along, but if it would get Ralph off his back, he'd go over there.

They drove over after dinner, while it was still light out. It was a tiny little brick building, one of the smaller branches, with a parking lot on three sides and the aforementioned alleyway in back.

"The place is the size of my bathroom," Larry said as they parked across the street. "What the hell do you think we're gonna find in there? Some kid's piggybank?"

"Bullshit, there's plenty of money in there. Cash going in and out, all day long."

Larry didn't bother asking for Frank's opinion. He was in the back seat, barely even paying attention.

"Wall's made of brick. We're going to need a bigger drill," Ralph said.

"The drill again. We're going to need a fucking bulldozer, for Chrissake. Do they have those in the Sears catalog?"

"Shut the fuck up. You're not exactly helping here, you know."

"Ralph, be serious for a second," Larry said, grabbing his shoulder and trying to shake some sense into him. "Even if we have plenty of privacy back there, do you really think we're going to be able to get in and out in any reasonable amount of time? This is Hackensack, you realize. It's a pretty big town. Cars going by at all hours of the day and night, and cops all over the place. How long is this whole operation supposed to take, start to finish?"

"Depends on the size of the drill."

Larry collapsed back in the seat. That was the end of *that* conversation.

***

It was Thursday night at Willy's. They'd driven over together in Ralph's car. As they went inside, Larry caught his foot on the doorsill for about the hundredth time and went flying, almost taking Frank down with him.

"Jesus Christ, Larry. Have you ever thought about getting glasses?" Ralph said, watching him sail across the floor.

They went and sat down. The teenyboppers were out in full force for some reason, like they'd come out of their burrows twenty-four hours too early. The noise was bothersome but Ralph was taking no notice of it.

"How'd the big date go?" he asked Larry.

"Boring. Like talking to the wall. And she was a prude on top of it, wouldn't put out at all. I don't want any chick that won't sleep with me on the first date. Too big of an investment."

"Classy."

Ralph was looking at him funny, pointedly staring.

"*What*?"

"So?"

"So, what?"

So, whaddya think?"

"About - " then he realized. "Oh, that. What do I think? I still think you're nuts."

"No you don't."

Larry glared at him balefully. "Drink your beer." But Ralph was still smirking. He wasn't going to let it go.

"You don't. I can tell, you actually wanna do this thing as much as I do. You can't hide anything from me, you know. I've known you since like before we were both born. I know you like the back of my hand. Better than you know yourself."

"Do you, now."

Yes, I do."

"For example?"

"For example, I know that whenever you hesitate a little before saying no, it always winds up meaning yes," Ralph said, grinning from ear to ear like a lunatic.

"Yeah right, you're so full of shit," Larry said. After a slight hesitation.

Larry took it home with him that night. The stupid bastard had really implanted it in his brain, it was like the power of suggestion or some shit like that. The next night it was Friday and the crowd was even worse. Frank was there with them, looking glum as usual. He was still in his funk, and was working diligently on getting stone drunk. He was getting drunk more and more often these days.

"You thought about it all night, didn't you?" Ralph said, shouting over the din to make himself heard as they sat at their usual spot at the bar.

"Fuck you," Larry said.

"Come on, enough dicking around. Are we gonna do this or what? Look, think about it this way - what do we have to lose?"

"Years off our lives," Larry said, but almost too quietly to hear this time. He stared into his bottle, a thousand miles away.

"Okay screw it. Let's do it," he said.

"What?"

"I said, let's do it. You only live once."

Ralph whooped like a little kid scoring a touchdown, then went dancing around the room. He came back and clapped Larry on the shoulder.

"Goin' to the can," he said, and did so, skipping off lightly.

"You just might be," Larry said under his breath.

Frank looked over with glazed eyes.

"We're gonna rob the bank," Larry told him. Frank's expression didn't change.

"Did you hear what I said? We're gonna rob the bank."

Frank shrugged like someone had just told him his fly was down. He never said no to anything. Then again, he never said yes either.

***

Ralph immediately sprang into action. He went to Sears to get the drill. The one he wanted wasn't in stock, and since it hadn't really been big enough anyway he went looking for another one. The hardware store had something that looked like it might work. He took it home and showed it to the others.

"That's the drill?" Larry said, viewing it skeptically as it sat on the kitchen table. "Ralph, that's for doing shit around the house. We're not fixing the sink here."

"Sinks don't have screws, you dumbass," Ralph growled. "You said that before. Stop acting like you're mister handyman or something."

"You get the point though. That's not big enough. I mean it's not even close."

Ralph considered. "You're right. I think we just need one with a longer bit."

"It's not the length, it's the width. The wall is made out of brick. We need some real hardware here, a serious piece of machinery. It's not like we're just poking holes through sheet rock."

Ralph went back out and dug around some more. After some investigation, he found a place in Lodi that sold equipment to construction companies that had more of what they were looking for. It was a big old thing, this new drill, it weighed about as much as a dump truck and cost an arm and a leg, but it appeared it would do the job.

"Maybe," Larry said, scratching his chin. "We're still gonna need to make like a thousand holes, though. It's gonna take us all night."

"And we need that sledgehammer in your parents' garage. The long one, with the blue handle."

"When do we get the schematics?" Larry asked.

"Shut the fuck up," Ralph said.

Larry got serious again. "You know, I'm kind of worried about Frank coming along on this."

"Why?"

"Well, you haven't been spending as much time with him as I have, but he's been acting kind of strange lately. I mean, stranger than usual even. Obviously he doesn't say much, but he's not even responding to shit these days. It's like he's hypnotized or something."

"Oh, don't worry about it. That's just Frank. He's an odd duck, what can you say. He'll be fine."

"I don't know. You haven't known him as long as I have. He was never like that before."

"He definitely doesn't seem too happy in general these days," Ralph agreed.

"He's seriously down in the dumps."

"He needs to get laid."

"We should havepoo married him off to that chick from the other day. Gina's friend, the one that didn't talk either."

"Another mute, could you believe that?"

"Yeah, never saw that before."

"Didn't know chicks were ever that quiet."

"Me neither."

"It was almost weird."

"It was."

"All right, so when are we going to do this?" Ralph asked, changing the subject.

"You tell me, you're the big cheese here," Larry said. "The man with the plan. The grand poobah."

"I think we should do it in the Fall. Early Fall, like first week of October or something."

"Any particular reason?"

"Yeah. Weather's getting colder at night, less chance of anyone being out for a midnight stroll or anything like that."

"I don't think people take midnight strolls in Hackensack, Ralph."

"Yeah but you know what I mean. People stay inside when it's cold out. Less chance of complications."

"Okay, fine." Larry thought it over. "Hey, if we wait until the end of October, we could do it during Halloween. We could dress up like goblins or something, it would be like a natural disguise!"

"Wasn't that in some movie somewhere? Sounds like I've heard it somewhere before."

"Dunno, maybe."

"It's actually not a bad idea."

"I think the huge-ass drill would probably give us away."

"Yeah, you're right. Didn't think of that."

"That, and banks don't give out candy."

"No, they don't."

"Especially at midnight."

"True."

"Out the back."

"Mmm hmm."

"Through a huge gaping hole in the wall."

"Okay, forget the disguises." Larry steamed a bit. "But it would hide our identities, wouldn't it."

"I don't think the cops would have any trouble taking our masks off, Larry."

But what if they hadn't caught us yet? What if we were running away? Aha, got you there....."

"Three goblins running through the streets of Hackensack at midnight, fleeing from a bank with a fucking alarm going off. Seriously doubt the costumes would help."

"I thought the alarm wasn't supposed to go off."

"Okay smartass, so someone saw it and called it in."

"I thought there was no one outside at night in October."

"Keep it up, see what happens."

Larry chugged the rest of his beer. "I'm still worried about Frank, though," he said. "I don't know if we can count on him."

"Nah. Frank'll be fine."

"Maybe we should leave him out of it."

"Third guy might come in handy."

"Okay. But if he flakes out, don't say I didn't warn you."

They sat for awhile, not saying anything else, just staring at the wall. October was just around the corner.

***

There were still two weeks left until the big day. They were going to do it on a Monday, while everyone else was still recovering from the weekend. Ralph was climbing the walls. He drove around town, walked up and down the street for no good reason, bought coffee and then didn't drink it. He went to the movies with Gina. He sat at the kitchen table watching the clock, tearing his hair out, willing it to go faster and watching as it slowed down.

Larry was nervous. He was bitching about all the things that could go wrong, saying they were going to wind up in trouble. Ralph told him the possibility of it happening was bad enough without him dwelling on it so goddamn much. He tried to placate him with whatever he could think of to say, but there was just no settling him down. They needed to get it over with before Larry went full pussy and pulled out completely.

September drew to a close and the leaves were starting to change. Still one week left. Shit. They'd taken another few drives past the bank just to see if there was anything they'd missed. The drill was going to work fine, Ralph kept telling himself. They had everything all squared away, the sledge was already in the trunk, the car was running okay. A slight rattling in the nether regions, but nothing that sounded terminal. In a matter of days they'd all be rich men.

Gina came over. "Let's go to the beach this weekend. One more time before it really gets cold."

"Nah, I can't," Ralph said. "I've got something going on."

"Give me a break, what do you have going on? You don't have anything going on. You don't even have a job."

But Ralph wouldn't say anything else on the matter. Which was unusual. He was being shifty, Gina could sense it. She saw Larry at the bar the next day.

"What do you guys have going on this weekend?" she asked him, sidling up with a beer in her hand.

Larry sat up like he'd just been zapped with a taser. "What are you talking about?"

"I asked Ralph to go to the beach this weekend and he said you guys had something going on."

"Oh - that's nothing. He was just going to come over the house and help my folks with raking some leaves."

Larry was just as bad a liar as Ralph was. Now Gina's interest was thoroughly piqued. She went home and wondered what it could be, what the two of them were up to. She thought about asking Frank, but figured she probably wouldn't get anywhere there. Maybe he'd write it down for her if she asked him to.

The phone rang on Saturday night. Ralph picked it up.

"Ralph - what the hell are you guys up to? Why won't you tell me?" Gina yelled into the other end. She'd been out with her friends in the city and was drunk.

"Just some stuff, Gina. Don't worry about it."

"Raking leaves, right?"

"*What?*"

"Larry said you were raking leaves for his parents. At their house."

"Yeah - well, that was part of it."

"What was the other part?"

"Gina, stop harassing me. I'm too tired."

"I wanna come over."

"No, Gina. Seriously, I'm too tired."

"I'm coming over."

"Gina - "

She'd hung up the phone. A few minutes later she was there.

"Get me a beer, asshole."

Ralph was too beat to argue. He went into the kitchen and fetched a beer for her. She ignored the beer as Ralph went to hand it to her and jumped on top of him instead, tackling him onto the couch and sticking her tongue down his throat. Oh well, what the hell.

It was Sunday night. The day before. T-minus twenty four hours and counting. They were sitting around in Ralph's kitchen, brooding.

"Maybe we should have a dress rehearsal. Like, go over there and drive around, scout out the place one last time," Ralph said.

"No way," Larry said. "That's just what we need, some guy telling the cops he saw the same car circling round the place for days beforehand. Besides, what's going to happen - is the parking lot supposed to move or something?"

"Was just a thought," Ralph said.

He was on edge, testy. And with good reason. He was about to try robbing a bank along with two of the biggest knuckleheads the world had ever known. Maybe he should have gone ahead and done it by himself.

"Did you fill up the car with gas?" Larry asked him.

"Yes, I told you already. You've asked me that three times."

"And the sledge is still in the trunk?"

"No, it's in the refrigerator."

"And the drill is in there too?"

"Larry, shut the fuck up already. Yes, it's all in there. Just chill out a little bit, try to relax. Everything is gonna be fine."

"I seriously doubt it," Larry said, going back to his moping.

"You know - have you ever heard of the power of positive thinking? If you believe something will go well, then it will. It's all a question of willpower. Willpower, and a positive mindset."

"What's that supposed to be, my horoscope? What a bunch of happy horseshit. You sound like some fucking hippie or something. Some New Age guru. Things will go well if you remember to put gas in the car and bring everything we need along with us. That's when it'll go well."

Ralph didn't sleep at all that night. Not that he'd expected to. He sat around the apartment all day long, on pins and needles. The sky was overcast, full of lead. It looked like it was going to rain. If it rained, he was going to call the whole thing off. The phone rang.

"It looks like it's going to rain," Larry said.

"Thank you, Nostradamus."

"If it rains, we should call it off."

"No shit sherlock. What am I, stupid? Look, just be here at midnight and don't worry about the fucking rain." There were simultaneous clicks.

It rained for a few minutes later in the evening, but then it stopped and the skies dried up. At quarter past eleven, the three of them were gathered in Ralph's kitchen once again, drinking beers.

"One beer only. One beer, no more. Nobody's getting drunk tonight."

"Or we may not make it to the show," Larry added, smirking.

Ralph glowered at him. "That's right."

They finished their beers and threw the cans away. It was eleven thirty.

"All set?" Ralph asked. There were no objections. "Okay, then let's go do this thing."

They got in the car and headed out. Normally they would have taken Route 80 to get to Hackensack but tonight they were taking the back roads. The streets were dark and quiet, still slick from the rain. They snaked along their surreptitious route under cover of night, taking different side streets, going this way and that, and then about twenty minutes later they were sitting in front of the bank.

"Park the car around back," Larry said.

"I know that, dipshit, we already talked about it."

Ralph slid the car around and parked around back. Everything was still quiet, no one else around. They got the shit out of the trunk and headed over to the wall. The drill was heavy as a motherfucker, even heavier than it had been before, they practically had to drag it along the ground to get it there. Ralph lugged it into place and lifted it up with great effort. Larry had already tripped once getting out of the car and was still stumbling around in the puddles behind them. He came over and leaned into Ralph as he began to drill, putting his hand on his back.

"Larry, get your fucking hand out of my ass," Ralph said.

The drill started working its magic, humming along and pushing steadily forward into the wall. It was heavy as hell though and Ralph's strength was already flagging.

"Frank, give me a hand with this thing, will ya."

Frank came over to help support it. Ralph gritted his teeth with the strain. Larry kept leaning into him uselessly and it took all of Ralph's effort not to heave the drill at him. Finally after an eternity they had one hole made.

"I told you, this is gonna take all night," Larry said.

"No it isn't. It wasn't that long, it just felt that way."

They put a second hole through, then a third. Progress was being made after all. Every so often Ralph looked around to make sure the coast was still clear, and so far they were golden. Soon they had a nice little ring of holes going in a rough circle, circumscribing an area big enough for a man to crawl through.

"Go get the sledge," Ralph told Larry.

Larry went to get it and caught his foot on something and almost went flying again.

"All right, just go sit down somewhere if you can't handle it," Ralph seethed. "You and that fuckin' splashing. Frank, you get it."

"Here it is, shithead," Larry said, sweating with the effort.

They were all sweating, in fact, in spite of the chill in the air. It was pouring down Ralph's forehead and into his eyes, and had already soaked right through his shirt. Even Frank looked a little hot under the collar. A few more holes and they were ready.

"Punch it out. Use the sledge," Larry whispered.

"Shut the fuck up, I'm working on it," Ralph said.

He smacked the compromised section of wall and it made one hell of a noise, a sharp report that went echoing all over town.

"Jesus Christ," Ralph said. "That was loud."

"More holes," Larry suggested. Ralph shot him daggers in the dark.

Yet a few more holes and Ralph's arms felt like they were about to fall off. He couldn't hold the drill up another second longer if he tried. He stepped back, picked up the sledgehammer again and gave the wall another good whack. It went off like a gunshot again but the wall gave a little shiver this time. It looked about ready to concede.

"Punch it," Larry said.

"I'm gonna punch you," Ralph said, hitting it again.

Another few shots with the sledge and the section of brick gave way, collapsing forward into the hole.

A deafening burst of noise split the air, screaming into the night from nowhere like some siren from hell, a keening wail that sounded loud enough to wake people up in Poughkeepsie.

"You fucking idiot," Larry said, almost too disgusted to care. "No alarms, eh."

For a moment, Ralph was disabled. His head wanted to go in all directions at once, he couldn't hold it still. The old familiar static electricity was shooting through his body and soon the alarms ringing in his head were rivaling the one going off outside. In his confusion he caught a glimpse of Frank, who was similarly malfunctioning, looking like a cornered rabbit as he tried to scamper forward, backward and sideways all at the same time.

"Get the drill," Ralph said, coming to his senses. He took the sledge and flung it over the fence.

"Forget the fucking drill!" Larry said. "Let's get outta here!"

"We have to take the drill. It has fingerprints on it."

"Throw it in the puddle, they'll wash off."

There was a huge puddle just to one side of the fence, a pothole that looked deep enough to swallow a small country. They each grabbed ahold of one end of the drill and shuffled it towards the hole. Frank joined in and made a clusterfuck out of it and the drill slipped out of their hands and landed on Ralph's foot. Ralph howled, seeing stars. He spun around and swung at Larry's head. Larry ducked and tackled Ralph and they rolled around on the ground for awhile, spitting and cursing. Frank stood hopping from foot to foot, impatiently waiting for them to finish.

The drill made it into the hole and then the three of them went for the car at once. They were scrambling so fast that they'd become disoriented however, flailing blindly in the dark and bouncing off one another as if they were pinballs in a machine. Larry made a left and went skittering down the sidewalk like an injured crab, while Frank went right, mistimed the turn, ran into the wall and fell over.

"Get your ass up Frank, stop screwing around," Ralph said coming from behind, lifting him up by the arms and redirecting him.

Finally all three of them converged on the car and they peeled out, shooting off down the street with engines roaring and tires smoking.

"The alarm went off! I knew it would happen! I just knew it!" Larry fumed.

"They must have gotten it fixed," Ralph said, still breathing heavily, wiping the sweat from his eyes and trying to concentrate on the road flying under their wheels.

"Either that or your buddy at the bar had his head up his ass," Larry said. "I bet I know which one it was."

"Doesn't matter now."

They blew one red light after another, went careening around corners and flying down side streets. They were only about ten minutes from home when suddenly the car started making a noise. It was the same rattling noise as before, only louder this time and mixed with more of a shudder. The noise got louder and louder and then the engine stalled out. The car ground to a halt.

"HOLY SHIT!" Ralph screamed. "OF ALL THE TIMES FOR THIS TO HAPPEN!!"

He turned the key in the ignition one more time and nothing improved. Ralph beat his head against the steering wheel, he clawed at the dashboard, he hurled heartfelt and imaginative curses at the sky. The lightning went coursing through his body and there were atomic bombs going off in his head.

"Get the fuck out!" Larry shouted. "We have to leave it here!" Ralph wasn't going anywhere, he wasn't done screaming. "Ralph, come on!!"

Two of the three were out of the car in a flash and were instantly sprinting down the street. Ralph got out and followed them and was soon hot on their trail. The night was completely still save for the rapid clomping of panicked footsteps. As they ran down the sidewalk, Ralph tried listening for the sound of sirens but couldn't hear any - there, maybe that was one, way off in the distance. With all the buzzing and thudding in his ears though, he couldn't be sure either way.

It was one thirty before they'd made it back to Bloomfield Avenue. They were exhausted, completely spent from the long marathon run. Larry went one way and Frank went another and Ralph a third and soon they were all safely tucked away in their beds. Ralph huddled underneath the blankets, afraid to move, too spooked to even drink a beer. He was still listening for the sirens. What a fucking day.

No sleep was had that night. At eight o' clock in the morning Ralph was on the phone with a towing company and at ten he was down there to meet them. And lo and behold, the car was still right where they'd left it, sitting parked neatly up against the curb. At least he'd had the sense to steer it off to the side before it had conked out completely - middle of the road would have drawn a fair bit more attention. Ralph looked around nervously as the winch pulled the car up onto the bed of the truck. There were no cops around, no people, no nothing. Apart from him and the tow truck, it was just as quiet as the night before. Maybe they'd gotten away with it.

The car went to the garage and Ralph went home. He opened the fridge, pulled out a six pack and drank the whole thing in one go. He was too nervous to call Larry, too nervous to turn the news on, too nervous to do anything at all. He got drunk and waited.

Larry came by later in the day. "Did you get the car squared away?" he asked, looking like he was dreading the response. Ralph was just sobering up.

"Yeah, got it towed to Isaac's," he said, rubbing his aching temples.

"Nobody around, no trouble?"

"No. Nobody there at all. Have you heard from Frank?" Larry looked at him.

"Have you seen Frank?"

"No, he hasn't been by. So what do we do now?"

"Nothing. We don't do anything at all. We sit around on our asses and do everything just the same as we always did it before. And if we're lucky, that'll be the end of it."

So they waited around and nothing else happened. No cops showing up at the door, no phones ringing with questions about where anyone was on such and such a night last week, nothing like that at all. And yet Ralph couldn't stop thinking about it. He obsessed over it daily, worrying both night and day, paranoid to the point of fullblown delusion. He heard strange sounds around the apartment, imagined he heard doorbells ringing when there were none, woke up in the middle of the night with sweat pouring down his face like some kind of terminal patient. He had visions of jail cells a mile wide, of manacles as tight as beartraps, of police cars the size of houses, fearsome harbingers of doom that went racing through his waking nightmares like some satanic Indy 500. If things kept up like that, he was going to lose what was left of his mind completely. He felt like that guy in Crime and Punishment, by

Dosta-what's-his-name, that book they'd made them read in English class one time, where the main character worries so much about the crime he's committed that he winds up going all soft in the head. Or something like that, Ralph hadn't really read the thing.

But as the weeks peeled off the calendar, the fears gradually subsided. Each day that passed gave everyone a little more peace of mind. Life went back to normal. It was November now, and cold. Frank hadn't left his mother's house in a month. Finally they got him outside and dragged him down to Willy's.

"Wonder what ever became of that drill," Larry asked, keeping his voice low. He looked around. Henry was down at the other end of the bar.

"Probably still right where we left it," Ralph said. "That pothole was about as deep as Lake Michigan. It probably stays full of water year round."

"And the sledge?"

Ralph shrugged. "Dude living in that house probably took it inside and kept it."

"Yeah right," Larry said, rolling his eyes. "A sledgehammer appears in his backyard the night the bank next door is robbed. He's really gonna just run off with it."

"Maybe he's in jail for it right now. Look, how the hell do I know. I don't care what happened to the sledge, and I don't want to know. All I care about is whether they come to bother me about it or not."

Ralph turned to Frank. "So Frank, how does the world look after months in captivity?"

Frank smiled and took a sip of his beer. If nothing else, the little escapade had knocked him out of the bad mood he'd been in lately. He looked back to his usual self.

"Has Gina said anything else about it?" Larry asked.

"Nope. Not a peep. Hopefully it stays that way," Ralph said. And as long as you keep your mouth shut, it should, he thought to himself. "Henry," he called down the bar. "Three shots of Jack."

The drinks arrived. Once Henry was out of earshot again, Ralph picked his up and proposed a toast. "To remaining above ground," he said. They clinked glasses and put the shots down.

"Hear, hear." said Larry. "And let's never try that shit again."

"Quitters never win, you know."

"Very funny."

"I think we should try again next month." Larry appeared ready to get violent.

"Just kidding," Ralph said.

Frank was gagging. Jack never agreed with him.

So things were back to normal again. Ralph and Larry and Frank were up to their old tricks, in the bars more often than out of them, getting drunk and killing time and waiting for the end of the world, just as if nothing had ever happened. The weather turned even colder. Christmas came and Ralph went to his parents' house and endured it and then New Year's came and that was over with and then it was the dead of winter. Even less to do. No more lawns to mow. Ralph hibernated in the apartment and waited for Spring.

Gina came by now and then, whenever the mood struck. Nothing had changed there either. She hadn't mentioned anything about the bank thing at all, which Ralph found more than a bit strange. He could tell she suspected something but she was keeping mum, as if she were staying away from the subject on purpose. It wasn't like Gina to keep quiet about anything. In fact, it was impossible. Then one night she finally spoke up.

"Ralph - what was it you guys were doing that weekend, that time when you and Larry wouldn't tell me what was going on?" she asked, draped all over the couch like part of the upholstery.

"What weekend?" Ralph asked, playing dumb.

They'd run a teeny-tiny article in the paper about the attempted robbery afterwards but it had been buried way in the back, and anyway Gina never read the paper so there was no problem there. Or was there.

"There's something you're not telling me," she said. She was smirking a little, her voice quiet and brimming with curiosity.

"No there isn't, Gina."

"Yes there is. And I don't like it."

Ralph drank his beer by way of response.

"Larry made that crack at the bar about you wanting to rob a bank. And then that weekend, someone tried to break into a place over in Hackensack." A long, pregnant pause. "Was that you?"

Jesus Christ. Well I'll be damned. How could she possibly have known about it. Through a friend? He didn't see how. She had exactly two friends, and one of them couldn't speak and the other couldn't read. Ralph looked out the window.

"I can see it in your eyes," Gina said, starting to laugh and poking at him with her foot. "You can't hide anything from me. That was you guys, wasn't it? You dirty little bastards, you actually tried it, didn't you. I don't believe it..."

Ralph headed for the kitchen. "Do you want another beer?"

"Yes please," Gina said, coyly. "Well, now I have some dirt on you, don't I. I'll have to decide what I want to do with it."

"Gina, stop running your mouth please. I don't know what you're talking about," Ralph said. He tossed the beer can in her lap and sat down next to her. The second playoff game was just coming on and he made a show of rummaging around in the cushions looking for the clicker.

Gina just kept staring at him as the Bears marched across the fifty yard line, the corners of her mouth twitching, her head waggling back and forth ever so slightly. "You dirty little bastards."

***

"Gina knows," Ralph said.

"Gina knows?" Larry said. "What do you mean?"

"She found out about it somehow. I'm guessing that someone at work told her about it."

"How would someone at work know about it?"

"There was a little article in the paper, way at the back. Like two days later. I told you about that already."

"Well, I'll be damned," Larry said.

"That's what I said," Ralph said.

The bar was empty but the jukebox was on. Frank wasn't there. They didn't know why.

"What did she say, exactly?"

"She mentioned your comment and then the thing in the paper, just sort of putting two and two together. I think she's actually smarter than we give her credit for."

"Women are dangerous creatures," Larry concluded, finishing his beer. "Ain't that right, Henry?"

"What's that?" Henry said, coming over and throwing the dishrag aside.
"That women are dangerous creatures", Larry repeated.
"Can't live with em, can't live without em," Henry philosophized.
"Have you tried the second one?" Ralph asked. Henry chuckled.
"Ever married, Henry?"
"Yup. Before the Civil War, it was. Rita was a good woman."
"Would you do it the same way, if you had to do it all over again?"
"Absolutely. Wouldn't change a damn thing."
Henry wandered off. Ralph and Larry drank in silence.
"We're getting old, you know," Larry said.
"Speak for yourself," Ralph said.
No, but we are."
"You're right."
"We gotta quit with all this crazy shit and settle down, I suppose."

"Guess so."

"The real world sucks."

"So it does."

"And being middle-aged is even worse."

"We're not middle-aged yet Larry, gimme a break."

"Yeah but we're getting pretty damn close."

Ralph decided not to think about that one any further, at least not right now. Larry could be a real downer sometimes.

***

It was two days later. A decent crowd for a Tuesday.

"Frank, Gina knows," Larry said.

"About the bank," Ralph added, lowering his voice.

Frank's eyebrows went up, then went down. That was all.

"I doubt she's going to do anything about it," Larry said.

"If she does, we'll just knock her off and dump the body in the river."

"Maybe we should do that anyway."

"Might not be a bad idea."

"Nah, on second thought - Frank would be too upset."

Frank's eyebrows went up again.

Ralph turned back the other way. "You still dating that girl?" he asked. "Gina's friend, the bubblehead?"

"Yeah," Larry admitted, almost apologetically.

"No shit. She any good in the sack?"

"No idea, she won't put out. It's going on six months now. Some Catholic thing."

"Then why are you still dating her?"

"Dunno. Nothing better to do, I guess."

"Nah. She's a real piece of ass. Probably worth waiting for, if you ask me."

"No piece of ass is worth waiting six months. Frank, what do you think, should I break up with this chick or not?"

Frank shook his head no. That decided it. Larry would give it another six months.

***

The alarm went off. Ralph felt around for something to throw but couldn't locate any ammunition. He was getting up early that morning so that he could be the first one down at the temp agency, so that if anything new came along he'd be the one to get it. Rent was due and he was going to be short again.   God damn this miserable-ass cold cruel world.

He made himself coffee and then drove down to the temp agency. It was the same old story, yadda yadda, we'll call you when we have something. Go play in the mud some more and maybe we'll throw you a stick.

Ralph got another coffee and took it over to the park. It was icy cold out with snow on the ground and everything but he felt like sitting there anyway, just sitting on the bench and freezing, all by his lonesome. Change of scenery, change of pace, getting out of the apartment for an hour or two, maybe that's all it was. Whenever he came to the park these days, he always looked around for the old man he'd had the baseball conversation with, way back in the day when the weather had been nice and the sun was out and the birds were singing in the trees, but he never found him there. It felt like ages ago. He hoped the old feller was doing all right.

Larry came by for lunch. There was a thump down below and then Ralph was letting him inside.

"You hadn't hit the pole in awhile," Ralph remarked. For once he didn't go for beer; he wasn't in the mood for some reason.

"I didn't hit the pole," Larry said.

Ralph threw some leftover pizza on paper plates and handed one over.

"Any luck at the temp agency?" Larry asked.

"Nada," Ralph said, digging into his slice.

"So what you gonna do?"

"Rob another bank?"

"That's not even funny."

"I'm going into the city on Thursday," Ralph said with his mouth full. He meant to see his bookie, Larry knew that already.

"That's a fuckin' waste of time and you know it. You have worse luck than Roy Sullivan."

"Who's Roy Sullivan?"

"A park ranger who got struck by lightning seven times."

"How the hell do you know that?"

"I read."

"Bullshit. You've read like two books in your entire life."

"Yeah but I read shit on the internet. Anyways, forget about that - listen, why don't you let me talk to Pete down at the pizza place? I told you there are always openings down there, maybe they could hook you up with something."

"Nah, don't worry about it. I'll figure something out."

Larry didn't look convinced. Ralph finished his slice and started on the second one.

***

Ralph went to see his bookie on Thursday and laid a bunch of bets down. Football was wrapping up and so it was time for basketball and hockey now. He went home and watched half his teams win and half of them lose, and by the time all was said and done he'd broken even, almost exactly to the dollar. He went out and bought a slew of lottery tickets, even the ones with the rinky-dink little payouts, and didn't win a thing. Everything was pointless. He didn't know why he bothered.

The three of them were in the city on a Saturday night. They were starting out at Roscoes and then were supposed to be going someplace else, some bullshit fancy-ass bar, another one that Larry knew about. His new girlfriend was supposed to be meeting them there. Gina had said she might show up too. What fun.

Now it was Ralph's turn to be in a snit. He was going to get shitfaced that night and he didn't care who else was around, male, female, animal vegetable or mineral.

"Slow down there, skippy," Larry said, watching him guzzle about his fifth keg of beer.

"There's gotta be more to life than this, man," Ralph said, his speech already getting slurred. "You know what I mean? There's just gotta be more to it than this."

"There isn't," Larry said. "Get over it."

"It's all a crock of shit."

"And that'll never change, not in a million years. The whole trick is to learn to deal with it."

Ralph looked him over with distaste. Larry had on a nice collared shirt and a pair of jeans that didn't even have any holes in them. He was really laying it on thick for this new chick of his, it was obscene. Frank returned from the bathroom.

"Larry's getting a little full of himself these days, isn't he," Ralph grumbled at Frank, still staring into his beer. "Thinks he's hot shit and all just because he's getting laid on a regular basis. Wait a minute, he's not even getting laid. Makes it even worse, doesn't it?"

Frank abstained from weighing in on the debate. "Yeah, maybe you're right," Ralph said. "Maybe it's me."

They met the girls at the second place, Ralph got drunker still, Larry and Ralph had a fight going back to the subway and everyone went home. At least Larry's jeans had a few holes in them now, Ralph thought to himself as he passed out in bed.

***

A week later and his mood hadn't improved.

"I'm serious, though. What's the point of all this? I mean, we bust our asses all day long and work and slave away and what do we get in return?" Ralph said. "A whole lotta nothing, that's what."

"Two midlife crises in one year. That's gotta be some kind of record, " Larry responded.

"Come on. Go ahead and tell me I'm wrong."

Larry thought it over. "You're not wrong. But you're not right either. You're just looking at it all ass-backwards. Life is what you make of it, like the old saying goes."

"Oh, right - look who's in the self-help section now."

Larry laughed. "Yeah, you're right. Okay but what are you gonna do about it? You're not some trust fund kid. You're not gonna win the lottery." Ralph pushed his new tickets further down into his pocket. "I mean, you get on with it, right? What else are you supposed to do? You go down to the bar on Friday night, you get drunk, you have a few laughs, it's nice. Maybe you get married and have a few kids, have barbeques, go to little league games and shit. Take the wife down to the Caribbean. Buy a second car. Guys like us, that's about all we're gonna get. It's all we can expect."

"I dunno," Ralph said, scratching his head, still puzzling it out.

"Aaaaah.   Quit your bitching and order another round." Larry slapped him on the back way too hard and went for the jukebox. "Whaddya wanna hear?"

"Bluesy stuff."

"Bluesy stuff it is, for the depressed fucker in the front row."

Eight quarters later and the blues were there.

***

Three months passed and it was Spring again. The winter had actually been pretty mild and the weather had warmed up fast, way faster than usual. Maybe that was a good sign.

Then, miracle of miracles, Ralph got a call from a place about an IT job. Apparently these bozos hadn't gotten the memo and didn't know anything at all about what had happened. Two interviews later, Ralph had himself another brand new office job. The money was good and the work was steady. They made him wear a pager every now and then and it would go off at some random odd hour of the night and he'd have to go figure out what was wrong, but he couldn't complain really - there were no giant bosses of death or little Indians to misunderstand; everyone there was actually quite normal and nice.

Ralph got back in touch with Max and they started having lunch together regularly, about once a week or so. Life was as good as it had been in quite a long time. And, according to Larry, as good as it was likely to get.

* * *

It was about a month into baseball season and they were all going to the Mets game together. It was to be a triple date once again. They piled into Ralph's car and went across the bridge, wading through Manhattan and fighting their way into Queens, then they parked the car in the swarming lot and headed into the stadium. Gina bought a hat on the way in.

"Ooooh, hot dogs!" Beverly squealed. "I want one!"

Beverly was Larry's girl, it turned out she had a name. Ralph applied palm to forehead. Not this shit again. What was it with this chick and hot dogs.

They got food and drinks, found their seats and sat down. They were way up in the upper deck, way out in right field.

"I think I hear God talking," Larry said. "How much you say you paid for these tickets?"

"A lot less than for the ones down below," Ralph retorted.

"Everything's expensive these days," Larry said.

"Ralph, what kind of beer is this?" Gina yelled down from a few seats over. "It tastes like shit."

"Get it yourself next time," Ralph called back.

Turning around, he saw that Beverly was in deep commiseration with her friend, Frank's girl Lorraine. It looked like a one-way conversation. "So, when's the wedding?" he asked Larry in a muted voice.

"Not for a long time, buddy," Larry said, equally quietly. "Not for a looong time."

Ralph noticed that Larry hadn't used the word 'never'. That probably meant that the wedding was just around the corner.

The Mets lost the game 3-1. The girls went home and the guys went to the bar. Plenty of beer had been drunk, and there was now plenty more available. What a wonderful invention the bar was. The place was buzzing, there was a pretty good crowd, a nice little cross section too - male, female, younger, older, the works. Some new faces, a few they hadn't seen in years. The scene felt communal that night. Ralph liked it.

"Shots on me," Ralph said, plunking a fistful of twenties down on the bar.

"Shots on Ralph," Henry yelled to the crowd. A tumultuous cheer.

"Hey, you might get laid tonight," Larry said. "That is, if you're not getting hitched yourself."

Ralph did a double take, then realized Larry meant Gina.

"Don't be stupid. You know the answer to that one," he said.

"She's getting a little better looking with age."

"No she's not."

"Okay, maybe not. Still, she's got spunk."

"She's got problems."

"Who doesn't. Gina's got character, you've gotta give her that. And personality goes a long way, especially as you get older. Nobody looks good at sixty."

Ralph considered the ramifications. Someone came down to buy him a drink to thank him for the shots, and then a few more friendly pats on the back followed. Buy a round for the house and you were a folk hero for about a half an hour. Frank had disappeared. Ralph swiveled around on his stool and saw him wandering around by the pool table.

"Frank's feeling sociable tonight," Ralph said, watching him.

Larry turned around to follow the proceedings as well. Then, to their surprise, Frank picked up a stick and joined the game in progress, a trio of young kids who needed a fourth.

"Well look at that. I'll be damned," Larry said.

"Never seen him do that before," Ralph said, equally amazed. "Maybe he's finally coming out of his shell."

"Wouldn't that be something."

"Watch his lips for any signs of movement."

They spun back around to face the bar.

"How's the new job?"

"It's a job."

"Fair enough. Any good-looking girls there?"

"Nah. It's a goddamn sausage fest. They're all over in the marketing department."

"Nice to have a decent income again though, right?"

"I suppose. Then again, there's something to be said for sitting around in your underwear all day long. What about Frank, didn't you say he was looking around for something new?"

"Yeah, he's looking. The finding part is what's gonna be tricky. It doesn't help when you can't speak. I don't know how he ever got that job at the supermarket in the first place."

"Maybe his mother went down and did the interview for him. Told the guy her son had taken a vow of silence or something."

"Wonder if that would work."

Frank came back over, the game was done. "More shots," Ralph said. Henry brought three shots over.

"No, four, Henry. You do one with us."

"Thanks there, Ralph. Don't mind if I do."

The whiskey went into a fourth glass and they slammed them down in tandem.

"To your health," Henry said, then shuffled off to serve the big boisterous group that had just wandered in off the street.

Ralph looked around the room. The bar was practically full. The music was up loud and the lights were way down low, the neons were flashing away over in the window, the fans were blowing the air around overhead and the clicking of pool balls could just barely be heard over the steady hum of the crowd. There were lots of smiles and laughter, the genuine kind, and everyone was having a good time.

Then Ralph remembered he had to work the next day and it just about spoiled the whole thing for him. But only just. He recovered in time to fend off the bad spirits and quickly returned to his beer. The evening spun on and the drinks went down and everything was in its proper place. Larry was right, this was as good as it was going to get.

And that was fine.

COMING SOON

WATCH FOR PART 2 & 3
OF THE SCREWED TRILOGY.

1. Screwed
2. Being a Bum
3. Over the Hill